Fury

and the Mustangs

by ALBERT G. MILLER

Cover illustration by Lydia Rosier

SCHOLASTIC BOOK SERVICES

NEW YORK • TORONTO • LONDON • AUCKLAND • SYDNEY • TOKYO

ISBN 0-590-31294-4

Copyright © 1960 by Albert G. Miller. All rights reserved. This edition is published by Scholastic Book Services, a division of Scholastic Magazines, Inc., 50 West 44 Street, New York, N.Y. 10036, by arrangement with Holt, Rinehart and Winston.

12 11 10 9 8 7 6 5 4 3 2 1   12   0 1 2 3 4 5/8

Printed in the U. S. A.   06

Contents

Chapter 1
DEATH TO THE MUSTANGS

For almost an hour Fury had been steadily cantering along the narrow trail. The stallion's smooth gait and his quick, obedient responses to the rein made it hard for the alert boy on his back to remember that little more than a year ago this magnificent, black mount had been the savage ruler of a wild herd.

As they came to an opening in the trees along the ridge trail, Joey was able to look down across the valley and catch a brief glimpse of the Broken Wheel Ranch. In the distance, the buildings seemed like part of a miniature village. As Joey watched, he saw a tiny, moving dot. It was Jim Newton, striding out to the corral to inspect six mustang mares that had been rounded up earlier in the week and brought to the ranch. The boy's heart was warmed instantly by the sight of the man who had given him a new, exciting

1

life and had taken the place of the father he had never known.

Jim Newton was owner and operator of the Broken Wheel, a small outfit that sold young horses to cattlemen as working ponies and to rodeos as bucking stock. Jim was a tall, amiable young man who had flown with the Air Force before coming west and entering the horse-ranch business. Throughout the state he was known as an honest, reliable man to deal with, for when a horse bore the BW brand a buyer could be sure he was getting the best pony available.

Fury was the finest wild horse that Jim had ever captured. Early in the spring of the previous year, Jim and old Pete Wilkie, his foreman, had ridden into the hills to locate the mustangs that had spent the winter in the high country. Moving silently, they had come upon the herd grazing on the new, green grass. The nervous, anxious movements of the animals indicated that they were as timid as deer and would flee at the slightest alarm. The two mounted men sat in quiet excitement as a tall, jet-black stallion slowly, but watchfully, circled the herd. He was their leader — the most magnificent animal Jim and Pete had ever seen. After a moment, Jim's mount snorted softly. The stallion gave a warning whinny, and his mares jerked their heads up and stood still. The great black stared defiantly in the direction of the riders, then nipped one of his mares; she fled into the safety of the forest, followed by her companions. The stallion roared defiance at the two men, then wheeled and sped away to protect the herd.

It had been a major problem to lure and seize the stallion. Because of his tremendous speed and cunning, Jim and Pete could not get close enough to rope him, but finally they tricked him down from the highlands into captivity. From his violence when he was corraled, came his name Fury.

No human had been able to approach Fury until Joey had come to the Broken Wheel Ranch. The boy had been an orphan who lived at the Children's Home in the town at the lower end of the valley. Because of his deep devotion to horses, he had sneaked away to the BW to see the already famous stallion and had dumfounded Jim and Pete by immediately winning Fury's confidence. Later, Jim had adopted the boy, and Joey had come to live proudly on the ranch as Jim Newton's son. During the months that followed there was no doubting the fact that Fury was Joey's own possession, for no one but the boy had been able to make him listen to human reason. Finally, after love and complete trust had developed between them, Fury had permitted Joey to mount him. But even now, after fifteen months had passed, Joey was the stallion's only rider — Fury would allow no other boy or man upon his back.

Joey smiled as he peered across the valley and saw Jim enter the corral. Then, as he remembered the serious purpose of his mission, he slapped the rein and continued onward. As Fury followed the trail through the dry timber, Joey lowered his head to pass beneath an overhanging bough and noticed that his saddle was coated with a layer of fine, brown dust. With his forefinger he made the initial J on the pommel, and frowned at the thickness of the grit. It had been a dry summer all over the state. It was August now, and there had been no rainfall to speak of since the end of May. The rain gauge at the Headquarters Station of the Forest Service reported point-two-six, a little more than a quarter of an inch. The station higher in the mountains recorded only point-three-eight. Men who studied such drought conditions called it "fire weather."

During the first week of June, Bill Gibson, the firewarden, had called a mass meeting of the ranchers and their families and had spoken at length about the dangerous possibility of a major forest fire. Following the meeting, Joey and a number of his classmates had been appointed Junior Forest Rangers. It was their duty to ride along the ridge trails and into the canyons, on the lookout for signs of smoke or small blazes that could develop into forest fires.

On this hot, dry morning, Joey was riding his weekly fire patrol of the high trail. The ridge was thickly timbered in fir and pine, with a heavy growth of underbrush between the tall trunks. Joey had learned from the firewarden's lectures that even a small flame in the region could result in untold loss of timber and wildlife, and what would be even worse — human lives. Now, he turned his head from side to side as he rode along, examining the ground, bushes, and trees with a practiced eye.

Where the trail turned at a sharp angle, Fury swung around a rocky ledge, giving Joey a clear, unobstructed view of the sky to the north. His lips tightened as he saw an airplane, climbing steadily in wide circles. He recognized the plane immediately. It was the one hired by Mr. Barstow, a wealthy cattle-man from the south who had recently purchased a huge ranch up the valley. As Fury's ears caught the far-off throb of the engine he jerked his head up, and Joey felt a shudder pass through the stallion's body. He leaned forward and patted the dark, muscular neck.

"Easy, boy," he cautioned. "Calm down. You've heard that sound before."

Fury swiveled his left ear back and snorted.

"I mean it, Fury. That plane can't hurt you. It's a couple of miles away. It's just the noise that bothers you, that's all."

Fury snorted again and quickened his gait. The trail ahead was thickly wooded, and the sound of the engine soon died away. But as Jocy rode along, he felt his anger mounting. He knew that when the plane was flying for Mr. Barstow, it meant death to the wild horses who roamed the hills.

Mr. Barstow was out to capture and destroy the wild mustangs. As a cattle-raiser he was selfishly unwilling to share the grass of the free federal graz-ing land with the roving bands. In July he had hired a bush pilot to fly low over the ridges and seek out the wild herds. Whenever the pilot would locate a group of the rovers, he would dive and bank his plane over them to start them moving. In their terror they would race from the canyons and mountain refuges onto the flatlands. Often, after having been flushed into the open, they were shot from the air.

When the roundups from the air began, Barstow

hired a drifting cowhand named Chick Lacy and three rough helpers to capture the wild horses. Chick was a heartless brute whose method of subduing the mustangs was unbelievably cruel. Working from a moving jeep, he and his men would lasso a fleeing horse, then fasten a heavy rubber tire to the end of the rope. In agonized fright, the animal would pull the tire along the ground, until it finally dropped from exhaustion. In that condition the horse was dragged onto a truck carrying other broken horses, and driven to a cannery, to be processed into pet food.

Jim Newton, like other humane people of the valley, was against this cruel, senseless destruction of the mustangs. He himself thinned out the herds, but in doing so improved the breed, and there was no killing involved. He had protested to Mr. Barstow, but had been told by the cattleman to mind his own business.

Barstow claimed it was his legal right to capture and destroy the wild horses that were eating the grass on which his cattle fed. Tempers flared, but the roundups and killings continued. Each week the bush pilot took his plane into the air. When he flew out over the valley at a low altitude, all the animals, including Jim's horses, were terrified. Fury was especially fearful of the low-flying plane. Joey understood his stallion's terror and sympathized.

Since cutting back into the woods where the plane motor was no longer heard, Fury had calmed down a trifle, but Joey could sense that he was still wary. As they entered a slight clearing, the boy grasped the horn of the saddle, stood up in the stirrups, and scanned the sky. The plane was nowhere to be seen, and Joey hoped that it would not turn back and fly over the ridge trail. But suddenly a convulsive tremor passed through Fury's body, and as the horse flung his head back, Joey glimpsed the whites of his frightened eyes. For half a second Joey heard nothing — then with a sudden roar the plane thundered over the trail from the rear, only fifty feet above the ground.

Fury came to an abrupt stop in a cloud of dust, and Joey found himself flying through the air like a stone from a slingshot. By the time he had lifted his head from the pile of shale upon which he had landed, the plane was only a dying drone in the distance ahead, and Fury was attempting to match its speed in the opposite direction.

Jocy spat out a mouthful of dust. "Fury!" he cried. "Fury — come back!"

But even if he had been able to hear Joey's command, Fury would not have obeyed. The terrified stallion was racing back down the trail, headed for the safety of his corral at the Broken Wheel Ranch.

The bush pilot was in a playful mood that morning. After flying parallel to the ridge, he zoomed around the north end of the valley, then turned back and buzzed the Broken Wheel Ranch from the east. When the plane roared over at a low altitude, Pete was outside the barn, filling the water trough. The sound came with such unexpected suddenness that the old man pitched forward and almost fell into the trough. After recovering from his shock, he bounced up and down and shook his gnarled, brown fist at the receding plane.

"Dang you!" he shrieked. "Dang you! Dang you! Dang you!"

Jim Newton appeared at the door of the hayloft above Pete's head and looked across at the horses, frantically milling about in the corral. The six new mares were racing around the sides of the enclosure, madly seeking an opening.

"Dang you is right," Jim muttered. He wrapped his strong hands around the feed-loading rope and slid to the ground. "Come on, Pete — hurry!" He raced to the corral like a sprinter and vaulted the fence.

Pete made the distance in somewhat slower time, and crawled through the wooden rails, puffing like an engine. "Somethin's gotta be done, Jim," he wheezed. "This time we just gotta take action!"

"Never mind that," Jim called. "First, let's quiet these mares down before they kill themselves."

After twenty minutes of wrestling, cajoling and sweet-talk, Jim and Pete managed to get the animals into the barn stalls, where they stood spent and trembling. Pete shot the last bar into place and turned angrily to Jim. As he opened his mouth to speak, Jim held up his hand.

"Stow it, Pete. I know just what you're going to say."

"But dang it, Jim — "

"Danging it won't do a bit of good." Jim glanced at Pete's face, which was almost comic with rage. His eyes twinkled. "Come on, Pete, simmer down. You're as jumpy as these mares."

Pete ripped off his battered felt hat and slapped it against a feedbox. "It's no joke, Jim! It gits my back up! If that there contraption keeps a-zoomin' over here like it's been doin' an' that Barstow keeps killin' the mustangs, you're gonna be outa the horse-ranch business, an' I'm gonna be lookin' fer a job!"

Jim's rugged face grew stern. "You're right, Pete, it's not funny, and that's the truth. I've got to ride up and have another talk with Barstow."

Pete scratched the gray stubble on his chin and looked out at the sky. "That roarin' buzzard'll be snortin' around here till there ain't a healthy horse left in the valley. It's gittin' so bad, I'm beginnin' to think I'd git more peace if I lived in New York City."

Jim chuckled, despite his deep concern, and walked to the door of the barn. "I can just picture you working in New York City, Pete. You'd — " Suddenly he stopped short and pointed. "Look!"

"Huh?" Pete's eyes followed Jim's finger.

"It's Fury!" Jim was running toward the road. Pete started after him.

"His saddle's empty! Joey ain't ridin' him!"

Fury was racing across the meadow toward the ranch gate, his stirrups flapping like empty trousers on a line. As he neared Jim, he slowed down to a trot, then stopped and wheeled in excited circles, his long, black tail curling across his rump. Jim reached out and grabbed the bridle. "Settle down, Fury! Settle down!"

Pete panted up and caught the bridle on the opposite side. "Where's Joey?" he demanded. "What's happened to Joey?"

"Get my horse," Jim ordered. "I'll handle Fury."

While Jim struggled with the dancing stallion, Pete ran up to the barn, threw a saddle on Jim's roan, and led the horse out. Fury's great sides were still heaving, but Jim had him fairly well in hand.

"If Joey's hurt," Pete moaned, "I'll — " he raised his arms in a helpless gesture.

Jim nodded and dropped Fury's bridle. The stallion turned and ran a few steps toward the meadow, then turned again to look at the men. Jim knew this trick of Fury's. "He wants me to follow him." He vaulted into the roan's saddle. "You stay here, Pete. Don't go anywhere till I get back." He looked toward the west. "I mean — till we get back."

"Don't worry, I won't. Good luck, Jim."

Fury was already thirty yards away, jerking his head at Jim in a come-on gesture.

"Okay, Fury," Jim shouted, "get going! Take me to Joey!"

Fury gave a delighted whinny and raced out through the gate. Jim brought his knees in sharply, and the roan leaped out in pursuit of the black. Pete watched the racing horses until they were dots in the distance. Finally, with drooping shoulders, he shuffled slowly to the porch steps and sat down to wait.

Joey picked himself up and gingerly tried out his limbs. They all worked, but he noticed that his hands were cut. By crossing his eyes he could see something on the end of his nose. He dabbed at it with his handkerchief, which came away red. With one finger he touched his nose fearfully and wiggled it around. It was skinned but not broken. With the realization that he was not badly injured, his anxiety gave way to anger. "Doggone you, Fury," he muttered. "That sure was a heck of a way to treat a friend." After dusting himself off, he hitched up his blue jeans and started walking.

Joey had hiked about a mile down the trail when he heard hoofbeats around the bend ahead. He stood still and straddled the trail with his hands on his hips. In a moment, Fury galloped into view. Seeing his angry young master, he came to a quick halt, looked at Joey for a few seconds, then guiltily turned his head away.

"You traitor," Joey said bitterly. "You can't look me in the eye. And it's no wonder." Fury's long ears flattened back against his head. "You're yellow," Joey continued accusingly. "You're a plain, yellow — black horse!"

Fury twisted his neck around toward his rump, as if to make sure which color was correct. While the horse was inspecting himself, Jim Newton arrived and leaped to the ground.

"Joey! What happened?" He knelt down and wrapped his arms around the boy.

"It was Fury. Mr. Barstow's plane spooked him, and he threw me and took off."

"Are you okay? Are you hurt?" Jim was feeling Joey's arms and legs.

"No, I'm all right. My nose and hands got banged up, that's all."

Jim sighed with relief. "Pete and I were pretty worried when Fury came home without you."

Fury sidled up to Joey and scratched the ground with his right front hoof.

"Look at him," Joey scoffed. "He's ashamed."

Fury pushed his muzzle against Joey's shoulder and made a low, pleading sound, deep in his throat. Joey pulled away, peevishly.

"Don't try to make up with me. You're chicken, that's what you are. You're chicken and a — a deserter."

Fury raised his head and nuzzled Joey's cheek. Jim threw his head back and laughed.

"Don't be too tough on him, Joey. After all, he did change his mind and lead me back to you."

"Sure he did, Jim, but — " Joey sighed and looked at Fury. Fury rolled his lips back and tugged gently with his teeth at the boy's shirt collar. Joey broke into a broad grin and surrendered. "Okay, you big galoot — you win." He rubbed Fury's nose. "It was a dirty trick, but I forgive you."

Fury threw his head up and neighed delightedly.

"I'm sure glad you've relented," Jim said. "Otherwise we'd have had to ride double all the way back to the ranch. Okay — jump aboard Fury and let's move. I'm sure Pete's having conniption fits about you."

On the way down the trail they discussed the plane and the killing of the mustangs. Mr. Barstow's continuing determination to wipe out the wild herds called for another strong protest.

"I'll do it right after lunch," Jim decided. "I'll ride up to Barstow's layout and have a serious talk with him."

Joey looked up eagerly. "May I go with you?"

"I guess so, why not?"

"I've got a couple of things to say to that Mr.

Barstow myself," Joey said grimly. He slapped his rein. "Come on, Fury, let's hurry it up."

When they reached the flatland the horses broke into an easy gallop, and a short time later, to Pete's relief, the two riders passed through the gate of the Broken Wheel.

Chapter 2

TROUBLE AT THE BARSTOW RANCH

Now look here, Newton," Mr. Barstow blustered. "I told you before to keep your nose out of my affairs."

Determined not to lose his temper, Jim answered in a courteous, controlled voice. "I'm sure you meant it, sir, and it's never been my habit to interfere — "

"Well, you're certainly interfering now!" Barstow cut in.

"As I was about to say," Jim continued calmly, "your treatment of the mustangs has caused great concern throughout the valley. For that reason, I feel that it's high time we talked it over."

Barstow struck the fence post with his fist. "The concern of you and those others doesn't interest me in the least! So I suggest that you and Joey climb back into your saddles and ride home to the Broken Wheel. I've no time to waste on silly arguments — I'm a busy man. I've got a *big* ranch to run."

Jim caught the hidden meaning but was not offended. "Yes, Mr. Barstow, this is a big ranch all right. Any man in the valley would give his eyeteeth to own it." He turned to Joey. "How do you like it, Joey? Isn't it a beautiful layout?"

"Boy — it sure is." Joey swept his eyes around the ranch with frank admiration. There wasn't another outfit in the state to compare with it. The main house, the barn, the corrals, the bunkhouse — all were of the finest and most costly construction.

It was the second massive ranch that Barstow had owned in his lifetime. Five years before, back in his native state, he had brought in a number of oil wells and made a considerable fortune. After years of waiting and hoping, he had at last been able to realize his ambition to raise fine cattle. It had taken him a long time to build and develop a magnificent ranch on the prairie, fifty miles from his home town. When it was completed, he settled there with his wife and their young son, David.

A year later, his contented world was shattered by a sudden catastrophe. When a flash flood swept away a bridge over which Mrs. Barstow and David were driving, his wife was drowned. Although David's life was saved, he never regained his health. The following year, Barstow was advised by medical experts to remove his son to a higher and drier climate. Through his agents he learned of the valley where Joey and Jim Newton lived, and as it satisfied all the requirements for David's physical recovery, he sold his prairie home, bought the valley ranch, and brought David there to live.

Barstow was embittered by his tragedy. He felt that the world had turned against him, and he was determined to make his own way alone. He resented anyone who attempted to advise or help him, or who even tried to be neighborly. As a result, he had made no friends in the valley. His only interests lay in his ranch and his twelve-year-old son.

Because of his father's unyielding attitude, David Barstow was a lonely boy. Although he was small for his age and underweight, he had a warm, out-going personality. In the spring, when David enrolled at the valley school, Joey and his classmates formed an immediate liking for him. But after the term ended, David had little opportunity to see boys and girls of his own age, for his father never permitted him to invite his young friends to the ranch. When David received invitations to parties or barbecues, Barstow always refused them politely, explaining that his son was not well enough to go visiting. Meanwhile, the man almost devoured the boy with his own attentions. He showered David with the most expensive riding and sports equipment and took him on frequent hunting and fishing expeditions. But David continued to yearn for the companionship of people his own age.

As Joey was admiring the Barstow ranch, he saw David emerge from the house into the sunlight. "Hi, David!" he shouted.

David shaded his eyes. "Who is it?"

"Joey. Joey Newton."

"Joey? Oh, *boy!*" David grinned happily and raced down the path to join the group at the fence.

His father spoke to him anxiously. "Here now, son, take it easy. It won't do to overexert yourself. You know that."

"I forgot, Dad — I'm sorry." The boy seemed embarrassed by his father's exaggerated concern before visitors.

Jim tried to make him feel at ease by extending his hand. "Hello, David, I'm Jim Newton. Joey's told me a whole lot about you."

"He has?" David was pleased. He took Jim's hand and shook it warmly. "I'm sure glad to meet you, Mr. Newton." He turned to Joey, delightedly. "And, am I glad to see *you!* I haven't seen you since school closed." He looked sideways at his father and added desperately, "I haven't seen any of the kids."

Barstow looked up at the sky and frowned. "You'd better go in and get your hat, David. This sunlight is pretty strong."

David nodded. "I will, Dad, but first — please let me say hello to Fury. I haven't seen him, either, for a long time." He walked to Fury's side and stroked his neck, lovingly. Fury made a small, welcoming sound and brushed the boy lightly with his muzzle. David was delighted. "See that, Dad? He knows me. He likes me, too."

"He sure does," Joey said. "He remembers you from school."

David's eyes were wide with pleasure as he turned to his father. "Dad, I think Fury's the most wonderful horse in the whole world. And you know something? He was a wild stallion! Mr. Newton captured him last year, after he found him up in the mountains. Fury was guarding a whole herd of wild mares!"

Barstow caught Jim's eye and looked away quickly. "Yes, son, I know all about Fury. But right now I think you'd better go up to the house and — "

David was too excited to listen to his father. "What're you doing here at our place, Joey? Is my dad gonna buy some of Mr. Newton's horses?"

Joey shot a quick glance at Barstow. "Well — uh — not really. You see — uh — " Now it was Joey's turn to feel embarrassed. He looked to Jim for help.

"It isn't exactly business that brought us, David," Jim explained. "We rode up here to discuss a certain situation with your dad. It has to do with the mustangs."

"Oh," said David. "I — I know what you mean." Noticing that his father's face had suddenly grown stern, he flushed to the roots of his hair.

"Your dad doesn't understand!" Joey burst out with sudden vehemence. "Those wild horses have a right to live, but they're all being killed!"

"Joey!" Jim warned.

"I can't help it, Jim — they *are* being killed. And the way those men are doing it is cruel! David asked why we came, and I want to tell him the truth. Maybe he doesn't know what's really going on."

"But I do," David said miserably. "I know all about it."

"Do you?" Jim asked directly. "And what do you think?"

David's eyes filled with tears. "I — I think it's awful."

"Stop it!" Barstow roared. "Stop this foolish talk about the mustangs! Don't you see what you've done to David? You've got him all upset."

"I'm sorry," Jim said quietly. "Joey shouldn't have spoken that way in front of your son. But since he did — and David has expressed his opinion — let's continue."

"How can my boy have an opinion? He's only a child!" Barstow was trembling with rage, and beads of sweat stood out on his pink, bald head. "What's more, he's not strong. I won't allow him to listen to this senseless argument any longer!" He turned to his son and spoke in a low, forceful voice. "David — go up to the house." The boy hesitated. "At once, David!"

With an agonized glance at Jim and Joey, David turned and walked slowly up the path. The others watched him in silence until he disappeared into the house. The moment the door closed, Barstow whirled upon Joey.

"I hope you're satisfied! You've reduced a weak, high-strung boy to tears! If he should have a setback because of you, I'll hold you responsible!"

Jim cocked his left eyebrow and looked at the agitated rancher.

"It seems to me that if your boy *is* high strung, he comes by it naturally."

Barstow opened his mouth as if to make an angry retort, then wilted perceptibly, and closed it again. "I'm sorry," he muttered. "I have a quick temper."

He looked toward the house. "And David is my whole life."

"I can understand that," Jim said. "He seems like a fine boy. But even though he's only a child, as you say, it's obvious that he does have a poor opinion of your treatment of the mustangs. Now are you going to discuss the matter with us, or aren't you?"

Before Barstow could answer, the grinding of automobile gears was heard, and a jeep containing four men turned through the gate of the ranch. It roared up the road in a cloud of dust, heading at full speed toward Barstow and his visitors. Alarmed, Barstow raised a warning hand, but the jeep sped forward without swerving. When it was only ten feet from the group, it turned sharply onto the dry grass where the horses were standing.

"Fury!" Joey screamed. "Look out!"

Fury and Jim's roan threw their ears up and jumped sideways. The driver jammed on the brakes and stopped the vehicle within inches of the alarmed horses. Jim and Joey ran to the rearing animals and caught hold of their bridles. Barstow strode angrily to the jeep.

"What're you trying to do, Lacy — kill those horses?"

The driver looked up insolently. "That's what ya pay me fer, ain't it, boss — to kill hosses?" He spat out a matchstick, swung a long leg over the side of the jeep, and stepped out to the ground.

His three grimy partners, who had been riding on a pile of old tires in the truck body of the jeep, climbed out wearily and began collecting their gear.

From where Joey was standing, he could see that the tires were worn and scraped, as though they had been dragged along the ground.

"Okay, Jep," the driver drawled to one of his men, "you an' Slim an' Race done a good day's job. Now go on up an' shovel some grub inta yer fat bellies."

The men laughed and started up toward the bunkhouse. Chick Lacy, the jeep driver, glanced sleepily toward Jim and Joey. His eyes, which were expressionless and heavy-lidded, gave the impression that he was constantly bored and weary. Chick was a tall, slouching man. His face was sallow and angular; a broken nose was its most distinguishing feature. His faded blue denims were filthy and threadbare, and his black shirt was streaked with dust.

When the horses were quiet, Jim approached Chick with a firm, purposeful stride. Chick watched him coming and tossed his battered Stetson into the front seat of the jeep. Seeing the man at close range with his head uncovered, Jim noticed with surprise that his hair and eyebrows were inky black, in sharp contrast to his watery-gray eyes and fair skin.

"I think you need a few driving lessons, fella," Jim began.

Chick grunted. "Not from you I don't."

"If those brakes hadn't been so good, you might've injured those horses."

"That's right. So what's yer point, Mack?"

"My point is — you're lucky you didn't."

Chick held his hand out and shook it. "Look — I'm tremblin'." He took a match from behind his ear and thrust it between his square, yellow teeth. The match bobbed up and down as he spoke. "You're that Newton character — the hoss-rancher — right?"

Jim nodded. "And you're that Lacy character — the horse-*killer* — right?"

"Ya read me loud an' clear," Chick said. "An' I do real great at it. If ya don't believe I do great, ask the guy that pays me to do it." He turned to Barstow. "What about it, boss? Ain't I sensational?"

Barstow waved his hand impatiently, as if to dismiss the subject. "We're not going to discuss it. I've asked Newton and his boy to leave."

"A right smart idea," Chick said.

"I'm not leaving before we've had our talk," Jim announced flatly. "And right here at the beginning, Barstow, I want you to instruct that plane pilot to quit buzzing the ranches."

Barstow scowled. "Is he still doing that childish trick? I've ordered him to stop."

"Well, you'd better tell him again. A few hours ago he almost took the roof off my barn."

Joey had come down to join the group. "Not only that, Mr. Barstow. When I was riding fire patrol on top of the ridge this morning, he flew low over the trail and spooked Fury."

"That can't be helped, Joey," Barstow said. "It's his job to fly low up there."

Chick jerked his head toward Fury. "This Fury must be a mighty nervous nag, huh, kid?"

"*Nag?* Don't you dare call Fury a nag! He's a *stallion!*"

Chick shrugged. "Nag — stallion — what's the difference? He'd make jest as tasty dog food as any other hoss."

"Listen!" Joey burst out. "If you ever touched Fury, I'd — "

"All right, Joey," Jim said sternly, "nobody's going to touch Fury." He turned to Barstow. "Now — let's get to the point without any more sparring. Don't you realize that if you continue killing the mustangs, they'll soon be exterminated like the buffalo?"

"That would suit me fine," Barstow answered. "Those wild horses are a nuisance."

Jim sighed. "But you don't understand. The mustangs are a living symbol of the Old West. They're one of the natural heritages of our country. They've got to be protected." He pointed to the hills. "Before the white man came, there were millions of wild horses on ranges like that one up there. And according to the latest government estimates, there are only about twenty or thirty thousand left."

"There's even less'n that now," Chick said drowsily. "We got eleven of 'em this mornin', an' shipped 'em off to the bowwow factory."

Joey gasped in dismay. "*Eleven?* Jim — he can't *do* that!"

Jim held up his hand and continued speaking to Barstow. "Must you have *all* the grass for your own cattle? There's plenty of it on these ranges."

"And I'm telling you there isn't plenty!" Barstow shot back. "Maybe you don't know it, but one mustang eats twenty-five pounds of grass a day. That's enough to feed one cow or five sheep."

"I've heard that argument," Jim said. "Are there any others?"

"There are plenty of others, man. Those wild horses destroy fencing and run cattle away from water holes. They're ruining the range."

Jim shook his head. "I'm afraid you're seeing only one side of it. As a matter of fact, the mustangs actually help the range."

Barstow looked up in surprise. "What do you mean? How could they possibly help?"

"Well, I'll give you a few examples of how they do it." Jim ticked the points off on his fingers as he spoke. "In the winter they paw for forage in the snow. This uncovers feed for cattle which might otherwise starve to death. They also break the ice at water holes, and that keeps the cattle alive, too." He paused to let his statements sink in. "So much for the winter," he continued. "In the summer, the mustangs keep natural springs open. But the cattle close them by walking into them to drink. And here's my final point in favor of the mustangs, and it's very important. All year round, their manure reseeds and fertilizes the range." He looked Barstow squarely in the eye. "Well — now are you convinced that the mustangs are of some value?"

Barstow considered the question for a few seconds, then shook his head. "Newton, you can give me all the arguments in the book, but you can't change my mind. Those wild horses are eating the grass I need for my stock — so they've got to go."

"But, Mr. Barstow," Joey broke in, "it's cruel to torture them. And the *way* you're torturing them is crueler still!" His words burst forth in a torrent. "Look at those tires in the back of that jeep. How would you like one of them tied around *your* neck?"

Barstow reddened and spoke angrily to Jim. "You've got an impudent boy there, Newton. You may have given him a home, but you certainly haven't taught him any manners."

Jim stroked his chin. "Speaking of manners, Mr. Barstow, I haven't noticed any outstanding demonstration of neighborly courtesy since we rode through your gate awhile ago." His voice had an edge to it. "And speaking of giving boys a home, I think that's just about *all* you've given *your* boy — a roof over his head, but very little else."

Jim's statement had struck a tender spot, and Barstow's temper rose to the boiling point. "That's enough!" he roared. "Get off my ranch!"

"Very well," Jim said calmly. "But you're going to be facing a solid wall of antagonism if you don't stop this man Lacy here from torturing the mustangs to their knees."

Chick Lacy made a rude sound with his lips, lighted a cigarette with the match which he had been chewing, and tossed the flaming match into the grass which bordered the fence. Instantly, the dry grass burst into flame.

"You fool!" Barstow shouted. "Do you want to burn my fence down?"

Joey sprang forward and trampled out the spreading flames. When he was certain that there was no fire left in the black circle of burned grass, he shook an accusing finger at Chick Lacy.

"What'd you do that for? You oughta know better than to throw lighted matches on the ground. If the firewarden saw you do that, he'd really tell you off."

For the first time since his arrival, Chick Lacy dropped his mask of weary boredom. "Ya know somethin', ya crummy kid," he rasped, "yer beginnin' to bother me. What you need is a hard shot in the head." With his calloused knuckles he rapped Joey sharply on the crown of his skull.

As Joey cried out in pain, Jim pushed Barstow aside and moved quickly toward Lacy. But Fury, too, had seen Chick's action and heard Joey's outcry. Lowering his head, he darted forward and gave the horse-killer a butt in the seat of the pants which sent him sprawling. Lacy's nose dug a small furrow in the gravel of the road. Howling with rage, he sprang to his feet and ran back toward Fury, flailing his arms. Fury gave a deep stallion cry and rose to his hind legs. His slim forelegs ripped the air, only inches from his attacker's face. Lacy screamed and covered his face with his arms.

"Joey!" Jim cried. "Grab him!"

Joey grasped Fury's bridle and pulled him away from the cowering Chick Lacy. "Okay, Fury, take it easy," Joey commanded. "You've scared him enough."

By the time Fury was under control, Chick had jumped the fence and was making a beeline toward the bunkhouse. As he turned to make sure that he was not being pursued by the stallion, the others saw that blood was running from his nose, and that his long, black hair had fallen across his eyes.

"Well, Barstow," Jim said grimly, after Chick had disappeared into the bunkhouse, "have you anything more to say to us?"

"Just one thing," Barstow roared. "Get off my ranch and stay off!"

Jim shrugged. "Okay, Joey, you heard the man. Let's move."

They swung into their saddles and cantered down the road. As they passed through the gate and headed south, David Barstow watched them from his bedroom window until they were no longer visible. A moment later, when his father entered the room, the lonely boy flung himself upon the bed and buried his face in the pillow.

Chapter 3
THE RUSTLERS

Supper in the kitchen at the Broken Wheel was usually a pleasant occasion. On ordinary days, Jim, Pete, and Joey would talk quietly about ranch problems and the day's events while eating the fine, wholesome food that Pete prepared. The old foreman was an excellent cook and saw to it that there was plenty for second helpings. He was always as pleased as a female homemaker when Jim and Joey complimented him upon the tastiness of the meal. But on the evening of the trip to the Barstow ranch, everybody at the table seemed in poor spirits. To make matters worse, Pete burned the veal chops and overcooked the vegetables, so that nobody, including Pete himself, wanted seconds.

After hacking at his blackened chop, Joey pushed his plate aside and stared out the window. Jim tried bravely to down a few mouthfuls, but soon gave up in defeat. Finally, after trying to chew his own chop with his store teeth, Pete threw down his knife and fork in disgust.

"Goldern it!" he exclaimed. "This here grub ain't fit fer hogs, an' I'm the first one to admit it. I swear I et better stuff than this durin' the roundup of 1916, when the chuck-wagon got buried under a landslide, an' all we got to eat fer a week was fried porkypine an' boiled saddle-leather." Pete glared at his glum, silent meal partners, then snatched the plates from the table and scraped them into the garbage pail. They heard him muttering angrily to himself.

"Simmer down, Pete," Jim said, as the old man continued to grumble about his own cooking. "This is the first time you've ever dished up a poor meal in your life."

"Thanks fer the compliment," Pete snapped. "But if you don't stop that danged plane from buzzin' this here ranch, I ain't never gonna be able to concentrate on cookin' agin. I'll be so shook up, the on'y thing I'll be able to do is open a can of beans an' serve 'em stone cold."

When Jim and Joey had returned from Barstow's, Pete had met them on the front porch in a rage. He told them that soon after they had left the Broken Wheel, the plane had buzzed the ranch a second time. Even the horses in the barn had been jumping like fleas on a hot griddle.

"I don't think that will happen again," Jim had assured him. "Barstow seemed upset when I told him about the plane, and he said he'd given the pilot orders to quit it."

After scraping the supper plates, Pete ripped off

his gingham apron and flung it into a corner. "I bet Barstow tole that crazy pilot to fly low over the BW," he said accusingly. "He's jest mean enough."

"He sure is mean," Joey exclaimed bitterly. "And, Pete, you oughta see those four men he hired to capture the mustangs. Especially that Chick Lacy. He's the worst-looking one of the gang."

"Yer tellin' me," Pete muttered. "I seen 'em at the Crossroads a couple days ago on their day off. The whole four of 'em — Jep, Slim, Race, an' Chick. They was hangin' around Sam Jackson's store, botherin' the customers an' makin' wisecracks." He nudged Jim with his elbow. "Ya know what them fellers look like? Like actors in them western movies. Ya know what I mean? There's always the good guys an' the bad guys, an' Chick Lacy an' his crowd look like all the bad guys bunched together inta one big lump."

"I agree with you," Jim said. "But of course they'd have to be 'bad guys' to take money for torturing mustangs the way they do. No decent cowhand would accept that kind of a job."

"I'd git my gun an' plug all four of 'em," Pete said savagely. "That is, if they wouldn't hang me fer it." He frowned and rubbed his wrinkled throat.

Jim's eyes twinkled. "I think you've been seeing too many of those western movies, old-timer."

Joey, who was still hungry despite his agitated frame of mind, opened a box of graham crackers and placed it on the table.

Pete looked at Joey and scowled. "A fine state of affairs," he said reprovingly. "In this day an' age, with good food aplenty, a growin' boy's got to eat crackers an' call it supper." Noticing that both Jim and Joey had started to eat the square, brown wafers, he shrugged his shoulders and thrust his own hand into the box. For the next few minutes nothing was heard in the kitchen but the steady crunch-crunch of graham crackers.

"Jim," Joey said finally, "what're you going to do about Mr. Barstow? Can't you make him stop what he's doing?"

Jim wrinkled his forehead. "I'm going to try, Joey. In fact, a small group of us are already trying."

"Can't we git the politicians to make laws agin it?" Pete asked.

"We can certainly work toward legislation. I know that people in other western states have succeeded in getting laws passed. But they don't apply to lands under federal ownership. So it boils down to a need for legislation on a national basis."

Joey had been following Jim's explanation closely. "Does that mean that the Congress in Washington, D.C. has got to do it?"

"That's right — and it's a real big job. It means that thousands of humane, animal-loving people all over the country have got to get together and tell their lawmakers what they want." Jim stared through the window at the darkening range in the distance. "And you know something, Joey? When we Americans become stirred up *enough* over something fine and important, we have a whale of a lot of strength."

"You bet," Joey agreed. "Look at 1776. We sure got stirred up then."

"Wal," Pete said doubtfully, "what you say

sounds mighty fine an' patriotic, but the problem is — what kin *we* do? I mean us few people right here in this valley."

"We can organize," Jim answered. "As Joey just said, we did it in 1776 — only a comparative handful of people." He flung his arms out as if to encompass the country. "And now just look what's happened."

Pete grinned and pushed his chair back with a bang. His bright, blue eyes were sparkling. "Now yer *talkin'!*" he roared. "Jim — before you made that fine speech I was nigh ready to give up. But now I'm as full of fire an' fury as — as Fury is!" He opened the stove and lighted the broiler. "Joey," he called excitedly, "dig inta the icebox an' fetch me that big sirloin steak. I'm a-gonna cook us a dinner that'll keep us from feelin' hungry fer three solid weeks!"

"Now *you're* talking!" Joey shouted, patting his stomach.

During the week that followed, several evening mass meetings were held at the Broken Wheel Ranch. At each gathering, Jim explained the mustang problem to his ranch neighbors and aroused their interest in fighting for legal protection of the brutally exploited animals. Everyone agreed that county and state laws would have to come before federal laws, and a committee was formed to bring the matter to the attention of the county senator. A resolution was drawn up to request measures prohibiting the use of aircraft or motor vehicles in hunting wild horses.

While Jim Newton and the committee did not believe that the mustangs should be left completely alone, they hoped for a protective and rehabilitation program "with proper controls humanely carried out." They realized that, without controls, future generations of mustangs would be weakened through inbreeding and lack of feed and water; therefore, such a program was necessary. Their immediate purpose was to stop the torture of the wild horses by Barstow and other unfeeling cattlemen in neighboring valleys.

Although Barstow had been invited to attend the meetings at the BW to argue his side of the question, he refused to put in an appearance. Instead, he publicly announced his intention to oppose the committee by using every means at his disposal. Jim and his friends realized that they had a fight on their hands; but at least, having been "stirred up over something fine and important," a small group of Americans had begun the defense of the mustangs.

Over the weekend, after the committee was formed, an entirely different problem presented itself to the valley dwellers. Late Saturday night, three cow ponies were stolen from the corral at the Circle C, a good-sized ranch not far from the Broken Wheel. The sheriff and his deputies went to work before daylight, but could find no clues leading to the identity of the thieves or the whereabouts of the stolen horses. It was the first case of horse-stealing in the vicinity in eleven years, and the news caused great excitement.

"There's nothin' lower'n a hossthief," Pete told

Joey at Sunday breakfast. "I'd shore like to git my hands on them hombres."

"Why?" Joey asked. "What would you do to them if you did catch them?"

Pete glared at Joey over a forkful of sausage. "Whattaya mean, what would I do? There's a fool question if I ever heerd one. If I ever got my hands on a hossthief I'd — I'd — "

"You'd turn him over to the law," Jim said. "As any good citizen should."

"Wal — mebbe I would," Pete admitted grudgingly. He shook his fork under Jim's nose. "But in the old days we never waited aroun' fer no sheriff, an' that's the truth." He forked the sausage into his mouth and chewed vigorously.

"But these are new days, thank goodness," Jim pointed out. "Under our laws, a man is innocent until he's proved guilty. And that system saves a great many men from unjust punishment."

Joey had been fascinated by Pete's mention of rustling in the old days. "Tell me, Pete," he said excitedly, "did you ever hang a horsethief — I mean really and truly?"

"Wal — no — not me personally," Pete confessed. "But there was a couple times when I shore felt like it."

Jim poured himself a second cup of black coffee. "This theft from the Cricle C has me a little worried. I've been planning to drive up to Capitol City early tomorrow morning to sell our new stock. The trip would keep me away overnight. Now, I don't know whether to go or not."

"Why?" Joey wanted to know.

"Well, if those thieves are still around, you can't tell what might happen."

"Bushwa," Pete scoffed. "By this time I bet them rustlers're twenny or thirty miles from here. Prob'ly they're jest a couple of drifters that picked up them Circle C ponies on their way through the valley, an' kept on goin'."

"Yes, that's possible," Jim said thoughtfully. "On the other hand, maybe they trucked the stolen horses out of the valley and stayed around to pick up a few more."

"So what if they did stay around?" Pete demanded. "That oughtn't to keep you from goin' to Capitol City."

"He's right," Joey said. "Pete and I can take care of the ranch. We'll sleep with one eye open, won't we, Pete?"

"We shore will. So, Jim, suppose you quit worryin' an' git outa here tomorra mornin' like you planned."

Jim sat back and ran his fingers through his hair. "Well, to tell you the truth I ought to go. Tom Simpson canceled an important appointment to talk business with me. I'm pretty sure Tom will buy all thirty-five of our new mustangs after we get together on terms. And we could certainly use the money."

"Then what in tarnation're ya hemmin' an' hawin' about?" Pete said vigorously. "Ya gotta start fer Capitol City early in the mornin', so jest set yer alarm clock and go."

"Don't rush me, Pete," Jim said gently. "This

horse-stealing is a serious matter. If the thieves were bold enough to steal from the Circle C, they'd think nothing of running off some of our stock."

Pete bristled and threw down his napkin. "An' whattaya think I'd be doin' while they was runnin' off our stock? Makin' a pan of fudge, or somethin'?"

Jim smiled, despite his apprehension. Joey, too, was amused by Pete's resentment at not being trusted to look after the ranch during Jim's absence.

"Honest, Jim," Joey promised, "we'll both watch the BW like hawks while you're away. Fury will, too. He's just like a watchdog — even better. Believe me, if any rustlers come prowling around here, Fury'll sound the alarm."

Jim pushed back his chair and stood up. "Okay, partners, you've sold me. I'll go to Capitol City and leave the ranch in your care."

"Thanks," Pete said sarcastically. "Me an' Joey appreciate yer confidence. But you oughta decided that in the first place without all this fool talk."

"Right, as usual," Jim agreed, giving Pete a playful punch. "Come on, Joey, let's get out to the corrals and look after the new stock. Horses don't quit eating and drinking just because it's Sunday."

Shortly after one o'clock on Monday morning, three men wearing nylon stocking masks entered Mr. Barstow's main corral and quietly led six skittish cow ponies out toward the ranch gate. With the stolen horses trailing behind them on long halters, the thieves jogged along the flatland under a moonless sky for more than an hour until they finally reached the old wagon road that cut through the canyon at the base of Indian Mountain. They turned into the road and proceeded silently for a quarter of a mile, when the man at the head of the procession raised his hand with a lighted match in it as a signal to halt. He ground the flame out between his fingers and put the matchstick in his pocket. When all was still, save for the nervous pawing and snorting of the ponies, the leader gave a shrill whistle. Almost at once, two headlights blinked on and off, fifty yards down the road. The men slapped their reins and continued forward until they reached a large truck parked beneath a vault of overhanging trees. The driver was waiting in the darkness with the ramp lowered.

"What kept ya?" he growled in a low, impatient voice. "Yer almost an hour late."

"That's tough," snapped the masked leader.

"But I gotta git goin'. I gotta drive all night an' deliver this load before it gits light."

"Quit gripin'," the leader said. "You'll make it — maybe. An' if ya don't — that's your funeral, not ours."

"My funeral is right," the driver whined. He squinted through the gloom. "How many did ya pick up?"

"Six. Can ya git 'em all into this busted-down truck?"

"Sure, it can take eight. But how come only six?"

"We take all the risk — that's how come," the leader answered roughly. "Six is all we could grab from a layout like Barstow's. The only thing you gotta do is drive 'em away. Let's start loadin'."

When the stolen horses had been led onto the truck, the driver lifted the ramp and slid the bolts. "When're you guys gonna bring me another load?"

The leader grunted. "Who knows? That's up to the boss. Hey, how far ya drivin' tonight?"

"A hunnerd an' ten miles. Why?"

" 'Cause I'm lookin' out fer meself, that's why. If you sell these here critters too close to home base, me an' my pals might wind up in the jailhouse."

The driver snickered. "That's your funeral — not mine." He swung into the cab of the truck, started the motor, and drove off down the dusty, winding road.

The three horsethieves watched the red taillight until it disappeared around a curve. The roar of the motor sounded like distant thunder as it echoed from the canyon walls.

"Wal," said the leader when the sound had died away, "I guess that takes care of old man Barstow."

One of his companions laughed. "Yeah. That crummy old buzzard's in fer a big shock in the mornin', when he starts countin' his stock."

"He'll flip his wig," said the third member of the party. "An', man, I'd shore like to be around to see it. That Barstow's got so much dough he could buy hisself a million horses like them six. But I betcha he's gonna holler like a stuck pig."

The leader chuckled. "And how." He reached up and adjusted his bridle. "Wal, boys, this here's our second haul. How do ya like the racket so far?"

"Real great," said one of the men.

"Yeah," agreed the other. 'It shore beats workin' fer a livin'. I can hardly wait to pull the next job. When'll it be — tomorra night?"

"Don't ast me," said the leader. "Like that dopey driver jest said — that's up to the boss." He yawned. "Man, I need some shuteye. C'mon, let's git back."

The men climbed into their saddles and headed back down the road in single file. As they cantered along they stripped off their stocking masks and put them away in the pockets of their jeans. Soon after they reached the open range, the moon came out from behind the clouds and shone on their faces — faces that would have been recognized by quite a number of the valley people.

The horsethieves were Jep, Slim, and Race — the men who worked for Mr. Barstow as members of Chick Lacy's jeep crew.

At five o'clock in the morning, when Barstow discovered that his horses had been stolen, he reacted exactly as Race had predicted he would — he flipped his wig and hollered like a stuck pig. After telephoning the sheriff and instructing him to drive out immediately, he strode angrily to the bunkhouse and berated his ranch hands for having slept soundly while the rustlers had been at work. All of the men seemed sympathetic, including Jep, Slim, and Race. Jep, their leader of the night before, sleepily asked for particulars.

"How do I know the particulars?" Barstow raged. "I was asleep — like all the rest of you! But I should think that *some* of you men would have heard those animals being led out of the corral!"

"Come to think of it, Mr. Barstow," said Jep, with an innocent expression on his face, "I did hear a noise out there around — uh — oh, say one A.M."

"Then why in heaven's name didn't you go out and investigate?"

"I thought I might," Jep explained. "But while I was layin' here thinkin', danged if I din fall asleep agin."

Barstow glared at the man, then turned on his heel and stomped out of the bunkhouse. The three horse-thieves grinned and winked at each other and returned to their bunks. The other wranglers, who had ranch work to do, got dressed quickly and went out to the cookhouse to get breakfast.

Later, when the sheriff arrived to investigate the theft, Barstow managed to overcome his dislike for his fellow ranchers enough to loudly demand that the sheriff band them all together to help him retrieve his stolen horses. The sheriff assured the irate cattle-man that he and his deputies would take care of the matter and would welcome help from the ranchers.

Although only a few of Barstow's neighbors sympathized with him, they were properly disturbed and alarmed by the news of the rustlers' second visit. Pete and Joey heard the news over the telephone an hour after Jim had left for Capitol City.

"I'm glad Jim got outa here before he heard about

it," Pete told Joey. "If he knew them rustlers was still around he woulda called off his trip fer shore."

"That's right," Joey said gleefully. "Now we'll show him what you and I can do when it comes to protecting the Broken Wheel."

Chapter 4

THE RAID

The Crossroads was a tiny group of stores situated about nine miles south of the Broken Wheel Ranch. It was built for the convenience of the valley people, and saved them the longer trip to town when they needed fodder and small supplies in a hurry. The oldest and most popular shop at the Crossroads was Sam Jackson's General Store, which carried everything from hay, grain, and feed, to groceries, work clothing, patent medicines, soda pop, and penny candy.

Sam Jackson was a friendly old codger whom everybody loved. For twenty-one years his General Store had been open from five in the morning until six at night, and at all times his customers found him behind the counter, ready to give smiling service.

Early in the summer, Sam Jackson surprised everyone by announcing that he had decided to take a vacation during the entire month of August. As he had not had a holiday worth mentioning since the store opened, everyone admitted that his month's rest was long overdue. On the first of August, Sam departed for New York, leaving the store in charge of a man named Matt Castle. Castle had applied for the job in answer to an advertisement which Sam had placed in the Capitol City newspaper. He was a tall, thickset man of forty-two, and as he was efficient and pleasant, Sam Jackson's business prospered as usual. To those customers who were curious about Matt Castle's background, he explained that he had been in the wholesale grocery business in the Southwest, but had sought less taxing work because of ill health. To the valley people, he looked in the pink of condition, but, as he was a stranger, nobody was rude enough to ask him personal questions. Everyone settled for the rumor that his trouble was high blood pressure.

Except for Sam Jackson's absence, the only thing different about the store since Matt Castle had taken over was the fact that it had become a hangout for loungers. This was one thing that Sam had always discouraged, but Matt didn't seem to mind too much when drifters, or wranglers on their days off, came in and hung around for hours at a time. But in spite of Matt Castle's toleration of the idlers on the premises, people liked him for his genial disposition and his industrious management.

On Monday morning at five-thirty, on his way to Capitol City, Jim Newton parked the BW station wagon outside the General Store and went in to place an order. Matt Castle and the young clerk had just opened the place for the day's business. The clerk was mopping the floor, and Castle was in the office behind the store, checking his accounts.

"Howdy there, Mr. Newton," Castle shouted cheerily, when he saw Jim through the doorway. "You're on the road early this morning."

"That's right," Jim answered. "I've got a long way to go."

Matt Castle came out of the office and shook Jim's hand. "How're things out at the Broken Wheel?"

"Going along just fine, thanks, Mr. Castle."

The storekeeper became serious. "By the way — any news of those thieves who raided the Circle C on Saturday night?"

"None that I know of."

"Well, I guess they were just a bunch of hoodlums passing through."

Jim nodded. "That's my foreman's theory."

"Old Pete Wilkie? He was in here just a few days ago. He's a great character."

"He sure is," Jim agreed. "He and Joey convinced me that we're not in for a crime wave, so I decided it was safe to leave them in charge."

"You were right. Rustling on a large scale is a thing of the past. I'd say that whoever those horse-thieves were, they just hit the Circle C and kept on going." Castle picked up a pencil and an order pad. "Now, Mr. Newton, what can I do for you?"

"You can send a load of feed out to the Broken Wheel."

"A pleasure." Castle moistened the end of the pencil with his tongue. "How much do you need?"

"Enough to take care of thirty-five new head for a couple of days."

The storekeeper looked up quickly. "Thirty-five head?" He gave a low whistle. "What happened? You bring in a wild herd?"

"Yep — all healthy and hungry. Ought to make fine range horses."

"Those animals are lucky, if you ask me. If Barstow's men had caught them, they'd be dead by now."

Jim compressed his lips. "How right you are." He glanced at his watch. "Well, I've got to be on my way. About the feed — can you deliver it sometime tomorrow morning?"

"I sure can, Mr. Newton. Bright and early."

Jim started toward the door. "Pete and Joey will be there to receive it."

Castle's eyes widened. "Oh — you mean you won't be there yourself?"

Jim stopped on the front porch. "No, I'm heading for Capitol City. Won't be back till tomorrow afternoon."

"I see. You're going to sell the new horses, is that it?"

"That's it — if I can get my price."

"Well, good luck to you," Castle said. "Have a nice trip."

"Thanks."

Jim went down the steps and got into the station wagon. When it had disappeared beyond a rise in the road, Matt rubbed his hands together and called to the clerk.

"Bud, run over to the storehouse and check the

feed, will you? Mr. Newton gave me a pretty big order."

"Okay, Mr. Castle, right away."

After the clerk had left the store, Matt hurried back to the office, picked up the telephone and called a number. In a moment, a cautious voice answered.

"Yeah?"

"It's me," Castle said gruffly. "Can you talk?"

"Lemme check. . . . Yep, it's all clear. What's up?"

"Listen carefully," Matt said in a low whisper. "The BW — thirty-five new ones."

"Thirty-five? Wow! How many d'ya want?"

"All of them—tonight. You can run them off easy."

"With Newton there? Not a chance."

"Be quiet and listen," Castle rasped. "Newton won't be there. He's going to Capitol to sell them."

"Who will be there?" asked the voice.

"Just the old man and the boy. Like shooting fish in a barrel. I want them all. That's an order!"

"Okay, you're the boss. Wait a second — what about trucks?"

"No time to make arrangements for that big a shipment. We'll stake the horses out in the rendez-vous for a day. I'll meet you there at two A.M. Come down to the old road and wait for me."

"Okay."

"Have you got everything straight?"

"Don't worry — it's in the bag."

"All right," Castle continued. "Pass the word to the boys and brief them on their duties. I don't want any slip-ups. It must be smooth and quick, understand?"

"I savvy, boss."

"One more thing. There's a black stallion out there that should fetch a good, healthy price. I want him, too, if possible."

The man on the line hesitated. "Okay. He'll be tough to handle, but we'll give it a try. That all?"

"That's it."

Castle hung up the phone and returned to the store. A few minutes later, Mrs. Barton, who ran the dry goods store, rushed in and told him excitedly about the theft from the Barstow Ranch. She had heard about it from the sheriff's wife, and the news was spreading through the valley like a brush fire. Castle expressed the proper amount of surprise and indignation, and gave his opinion that with the sheriff on the job the rustlers would soon be caught.

After Mrs. Barton had hustled out to spread the story further, Matt Castle calmly proceeded to open a carton of canned goods. While he worked, he whistled. He was immensely pleased with himself.

Jep, Slim, and Race dismounted and tied their horses to the gate of the Broken Wheel. Working quickly, they slipped their stocking masks over their heads. The taut, black nylon distorted their features, causing them to resemble a trio of black-faced apes with flattened, twisted noses.

Jep glanced up at the faint moon and swore softly. "A moon," he grunted, "that's all we need. Let's go."

Staying on the grass to deaden the sound, the men loped toward the house. When they reached the steps, Race darted into the bushes and stood guard against trouble. Jep and Slim tiptoed stealthily forward to the barn. At the telephone box, Slim reached into his pocket and drew out a pair of wire cutters. As Jep bent over, Slim stepped onto his back, reached up and snipped the telephone line. Jep twisted his head upward and nodded in satisfaction at the dangling ends of wire. Slim stepped down and returned the wire cutters to his jeans.

"Okay," Jep whispered. "The black stallion's in the little corral. We'll get him out first, then run the others off in a bunch."

He beckoned, and Slim followed him across the gravel to Fury's enclosure. With their lariats ready, they opened the gate and moved quietly forward. When their boots crunched into the hardpan, Fury flung his head up and gave a loud snort. The two rustlers stopped in their tracks.

Slim was annoyed. "He'll wake up the old man."

"So what?" Jep said. He glanced toward the dark house. "Race can take care of that old monkey with one hand. C'mon — let's git two ropes around this black baby's neck."

As the men moved forward, Fury eyed them with suspicion. His ears were twitching, and his tail stood straight out. The men raised their ropes.

"Now!" Jep cried.

Both loops shot out and coiled above Fury's head. He bent his neck downward and leaped sideways. The loops missed his head by inches and fell to the ground. As the men hastily pulled in their limp lines, Fury turned toward the house and whinnied shrilly.

Joey, who had been sleeping lightly, heard Fury's call and sprang from his bed. As he reached the window, Fury repeated the warning sound. In the dim light, Joey saw the two figures moving quickly about the enclosure. Fury was darting from side to side, attempting to corner them.

"Pete!" Joey cried at the top of his voice. "Pete! Wake up!" He stepped into his shoes, grabbed his Levis, and darted from the bedroom. The telephone was on Jim's desk in the outer room. Joey felt for it in the darkness, found it and lifted the receiver. "Operator!" he shouted. "Operator!" There was no answer. He jiggled the hook desperately, then realized with fright that the phone was dead. "Pete!" he called. "Pete! Hurry!"

Pete's door swung open with a crash, and the old man came running out, frantically tucking his nightshirt into the waistband of his trousers. "What in tarnation's goin' on?" he demanded.

"The rustlers! They're in Fury's corral!"

"Holy Hannah!" Pete exploded. "Call the sheriff!"

"I can't — the phone's dead!"

Pete switched on the light. His grizzled face looked like a thunderhead. "You wait here!" he directed. "I'll fix them thievin' devils!" He jerked the front door open and padded across the porch in his carpet slippers. "Goldern you!" he shouted into the night. "What're you doin' on our ranch?" As he started down the wooden steps, Joey shot past him and sprinted toward the corral.

"Joey, come back here!" Pete shouted. "Joey! Come b — "

The rest of the command was cut off by a large hand slapped across Pete's mouth. Race had emerged from the bushes and attacked him from behind. Pete's hands shot up and grabbed Race's arm, but the younger, heavier man applied a bear hug, tossed him to the ground, and sat on his stomach.

Pete struggled to get out from under his attacker. "Lemme up!" he gasped. "Lemme up, durn ya!"

"Lay quiet, old man," said Race, "or I'll hafta conk ya one."

Pete was wheezing because of the weight on his chest. "Ya dirty coward! If ya hadn't jumped me from behind, I'd be sittin' on *your* stummick! An' take that stockin' off yer face — or is yer face too durn ugly to be seen?"

"Ya know somethin'," Race said. "I'm gittin' mighty tired of your squeakin'." He whipped out a handkerchief, slapped it across Pete's mouth and tied it securely behind his head. "Now we'll jest sit here till my pals're ready to move."

Down at Fury's corral, Jep and Slim leaped the fence, only inches ahead of the stallion's slashing hoofs.

"We can't handle that black devil," Jep called to Slim. "So let's head fer the big corral an' haze the herd out."

Joey stopped running when he saw the men, and crouched low against the fence until they were thirty yards away. Satisfied that he had not been seen, he snaked through the bars and called Fury softly. Fury whinnied and cantered to Joey's side. The big horse was breathing heavily and snorting with excitement. Joey laid his hands on the soft muzzle.

"Quiet down," he whispered. "Come on now — calm yourself." Fury stomped the ground nervously. "Please!" Joey begged. "Take it easy. We've got to get to a phone and call the sheriff." He took a few steps to the fence and lifted a hackamore from a post. Fury followed him and lowered his head. "Atta boy," Joey murmured. "Now just stand still, and let me put this on you." Obediently, Fury allowed the bridle to be slipped into place.

Suddenly, a gruff voice broke the stillness, just across the fence. "Nice work, kid."

Joey whirled and saw the tall figure in the terrifying black mask. It was Jep. He had seen Joey in the corral and had come back to investigate.

"That horse does jest what ya tellim to," Jep said. "So we'll jest let you ride him outa here fer us."

"No!" Joey said defiantly. "I won't do it!"

Jep drew a pistol from his belt and aimed it at Fury's head. "Ya better do like I say," he warned. "He won't be much good to nobody with a slug in his noggin." He barked an order to Slim, who had come down to see what was happening. "Git a blindfold on this kid."

"What fer?" Slim asked. "We don't want no kid around."

"Right. But he can ride this horse to the hideaway — then we can git rid of him. Savvy?"

"I see whatcha mean. C'mere, kid." Slim reached over the fence and grabbed Joey by the hair.

Fury bellowed with rage, but could do nothing to Slim because Joey stood between them. In a few seconds, Joey was securely blindfolded.

Five minutes later, Jep and Slim drove the thirty-five mustangs through the ranch gate, and hazed them across the open range toward the rendezvous. Race followed them more slowly, riding beside Fury and holding him close by a short halter. Joey sat silently upon Fury's back, unable to see because of his tight blindfold. But as he rode along, he listened intently to every sound.

Back at the ranch house, Pete lay squirming on the floor, attempting to loosen the ropes which bound his hands and feet.

Miles from the Broken Wheel Ranch, the rustlers had built a temporary corral at the end of a box canyon. Soon after the stolen horses had been driven inside, Race arrived with Fury and Joey, and led them into the enclosure. After dismounting, he slipped a noose around Fury's neck and tied him to a tree.

"Okay, kid," Race said, "this here's the enda the line. Git down off that horse."

Joey slid to the ground and, on a quick impulse, reached for his blindfold. Race grabbed his arms.

"No ya don't!" he snarled. "You ain't seein' nothin'." He picked Joey up and carried him outside the corral like a bundle of wash. "Hey," he said to Jep, "what'll we do with this wise kid?"

"We'll take him down the road. You wait here."

"Watch out he don't see nothin'."

Jep grunted. "He won't."

Joey strained his ears to pick up sounds as Jep and Slim led him along. He knew that he was walking on underbrush, then presently there was firm ground beneath his feet. It felt like a rutted road.

"Where are we?" Joey asked.

Slim laughed. "We ain't at the Broken Wheel Ranch."

Jep held Joey to one side and whispered to Slim. "You stay here with the kid. I'll go along the road and look fer the boss." He removed his mask and started down the road. After he had been walking for ten minutes, he saw the headlights of an approaching car. He stood still in the middle of the road, waving his arms. The car stopped and Jep ran toward it. The driver was Matt Castle.

"Well," Matt asked anxiously, "how did it go?"

"Great, boss — we got all thirty-five of Newton's horses."

"Good work."

Jep grinned. "I got news fer ya. We took the stallion, too."

Castle leaned out of the car. "Fury? That's wonderful. Which one of you rode him?"

"None of us *could* ride him. We made the kid do it."

Castle scowled. "You idiot! Did you bring that boy out here?"

"Keep yer shirt on," Jep said. "He was blindfolded. He still is."

"I don't care if he was blindfolded or not! You shouldn't have taken that risk! Where is he?"

Jep pointed. "Down the road with Slim. I was figgerin' on turnin' him loose — out on the range someplace."

Castle pounded the steering wheel. "You must have been out of your minds! Go back and get rid of him right away!"

"Okay. Where'll I dump him?"

Matt thought for a moment. "Leave him on the side of the road, down near the mill creek bridge. Tie his hands and feet."

"Okay, then what?"

"I'll drive by there in an hour or so and find him — by accident."

Jep nodded. "Okay — you're the boss."

"Now get going. I'll be in touch with you later."

Jep trudged back to Joey and Slim, and carried out his part of the plan. An hour and a quarter later, Joey was "discovered" by Matt Castle. Matt leaped from his car and ripped off the blindfold.

"Joey Newton!" he exclaimed, feigning amazement. "What on earth happened?"

"The rustlers!" Joey gasped. "They raided our ranch! They got Fury!"

Castle seemed enraged. "Those thieves tied you up and left you here?"

"That's right, Mr. Castle. We've got to get the sheriff!"

"Indeed we do." Castle was untying the ropes which bound Joey's arms and legs. "I was patrolling for the sheriff — that's why I drove out along this creek." He rubbed Joey's stiff wrists. "You're a lucky boy that I came along and found you."

"You said it." Joey jumped up and down to restore his circulation.

"We'll drive over to the store and call the sheriff," Castle said. "This time those horsethieves have gone too far!" He gave Joey a sideways glance. "By the way, Joey — you didn't recognize any of them, did you?"

"No, sir, that blindfold was really tight." Joey hobbled stiffly toward the car. "Come on, Mr. Castle, we've got to hurry! I don't know what happened to Pete, and — " his voice broke — "and those men have got Fury!"

Chapter 5
A COLD TRAIL

The instant Race had left to join the other rustlers, Pete began his attempt to free himself. He soon discovered that no amount of twisting or wrenching would loosen the hitch, and realized that the rope would have to be either cut or burned. As he swept his eyes around the room, looking for some object sharp enough to sever his bonds, he heard the roar of hoofbeats as the thirty-five horses were driven from the corral and out through the gate. A moment later he caught the sound of two more horses pounding the gravel, and after they, too, had passed through the gate and reached the grass of the meadow, a dead silence fell upon the Broken Wheel.

More alarmed for Joey than for the horses, Pete rolled across the floor until he reached the fireplace, where an iron kettle-hook projected from the wall. Raising his body to a sitting position, he slipped the bandana mouth gag over the hook and jerked his head back. The handkerchief ripped in two, freeing his mouth.

"Joey!" he called. "Joey! Are ya out there?"

He strained his ears, but heard no human reply. A coyote barked from the brush behind the house, and another one answered from far out on the range. With dread in his heart, Pete slithered his way to the kitchen, bridging his body along the floor like an inchworm. When he finally reached the gas stove, he rolled to his right side, bent his legs, and hitched himself first to his knees, then to his feet. Keeping his back to the stove, he was able to extend one finger and turn on the gas of the front burner. When the pilot light ignited the gas, he raised his wrists and slid them backward toward the burner until he could feel the heat of the flame. Closing his mind to the pain, he held his arms still until a feeble flicker of light and the stench of burning hemp told him that the rope had ignited. He allowed the rope to burn until the hair on his arms was singed, then he hopped forward and severed the flaming strands by bringing them down sharply upon the top slat of a metal chair. Hopping to the sink, he turned on the faucet and doused the smoldering fibers. With a kitchen knife he freed his feet, and cut the charred ends of rope from his wrists.

Within seconds he was in the barn, saddling a bald-faced sorrel, and an instant later he galloped through the gate, headed for the Allen ranch, his nearest neighbors.

The sheriff was out on night patrol when Pete reached his headquarters by telephone, but one of the deputies assured Pete that his chief had promised to check the office every hour. The deputy took down all the facts about the raid and told Pete to return home and await developments. Pete put up a strong argument, then admitted grudgingly that it was a wise plan. But before he left the phone he put in a long distance call to Jim at his hotel in Capitol City.

Jim was stunned when he heard the news of the raid and Joey's disappearance. He ordered Pete to go back to the Broken Wheel and wait there for the sheriff. He said that he, himself, would check out of the hotel immediately and, by driving all night, would arrive home in the morning.

Pete left the phone and rode back to the ranch with a heavy heart. After checking the ranch house and finding it empty, he remounted and rode out onto the meadow, calling Joey's name. His fruitless, zigzag search continued for more than an hour, and as he turned back toward the BW he saw the headlights of two automobiles spearing the darkness. Urging his horse into a gallop, he arrived at the house just after the cars had pulled up at the porch. He recognized them as belonging to the sheriff and Matt Castle.

"Sheriff!" he cried, leaping to the ground. "Did ya find Joey?"

A small figure emerged from Castle's car. "Here I am, Pete — I'm okay!"

"Thank the good Lord!" Pete said fervently. "Now if I could on'y git to Jim I could set *his* mind to rest."

"How does Jim know about it?" the sheriff asked.

"I phoned from the Allens' place. Got Jim outa bed. He's drivin' all night to git here."

"Poor Mr. Newton," Matt Castle said, with a great show of sympathy. "It's going to be an anxious trip for him — not knowing what's happened to Joey."

"I shore don't envy him," Pete said. "Jim loves this boy like his own son." He placed his free arm around Joey's shoulder. "What happened, boy?"

Prompted now and then by the sheriff and Castle, Joey blurted out the story of his adventure. He said that after Castle had found him at the side of the road, they had driven to the Crossroads and called the sheriff's office. They had waited at the store until the sheriff had been contacted, then all had driven out to the Broken Wheel together. Joey spoke almost hysterically when he told about the loss of Fury, and about his fears for the stallion's safety.

"We know just how you feel, Joey," the sheriff said gently. "But worrying won't help the situation. My men are already scouring the range, looking for the secret corral you told us about. When we find it, I'm sure Fury will be there, safe and sound."

Now that Joey was accounted for, Pete's anger boiled up like Old Faithful. "The confounded nerve of them rustlers!" he raged. "I ain't never seén nothin' to match it, Sheriff. We ain't had much range stock around her fer weeks till we brung in them thirty-five head! Then Jim goes to the city fer one night an' — whammy — we git raided!"

"It's an outrage," Matt Castle said with a long face. "What do you make of it, Sheriff?"

"I don't know, Mr. Castle, but it's obvious that the gang is well organized." He turned to Pete. "Since your phone was dead, I thought I'd better drive out here to check on you. Now that you're okay, I've got to join my men. We're going to ride all night."

Joey looked up eagerly. "Can Pete and I go with you?"

"Hold on there," Pete said. "The on'y place yore goin' right now is bed. Yer dead on yer feet."

"But, Pete!" Joey pleaded. "We've got to find Fury! We've just *got* to!"

The sheriff patted Joey on the shoulder. "Suppose you leave that to me, son. That's what I'm paid for. If the thieves aren't found by morning, everybody will be out searching."

"Yes, sir," Joey said sorrowfully. "But please promise to look real hard." He was so exhausted, his eyes were almost closed. "Good night, Mr. Castle," he murmured. "And thanks for all you did for me."

"Don't mention it, Joey," Castle said. "And don't worry about Fury. As the sheriff just told you, worrying won't help."

"Now s'pose you mosey on inside an' bed down," Pete advised. "You'll wanta be rarin' to go in the mornin' when Jim gits back."

"That's right. 'Night, everybody." Joey dragged himself up the steps and into the house. Once inside the door, he hesitated just long enough to hear what else the men might have to say.

Castle was speaking. "It's a tragic thing, Sheriff. If anything should happen to Fury it would break that boy's heart."

"I know," came the sheriff's voice. "But we'll find Fury and those other horses — if they're still in this area."

"That's jest it," Pete remarked. "What if them bandits already got them *outa* this area? Then what'll happen to 'em?"

"They'll be sold," the sheriff replied. "If they can find buyers who don't ask questions."

"An, if they can't sell 'em?" Pete queried.

"They'll do what Barstow does — take them to the slaughterhouse."

Joey clapped his hands over his ears and ran to his bedroom. In a few minutes he was asleep, but tortured by a dream that Fury was being driven blindfolded into a dark room filled with masked, jeering men.

Jim's face was weary and drawn as he listened to Pete's story. He had driven alone through the night, tormented by his fears for Joey. When he had heard from Pete that the boy was unharmed and in bed, his relief had been almost a shock. Pete brought him a pot of coffee, which Jim drank in silence as his foreman's angry tale unfolded.

"If that big feller hadn'ta jumped me from behind," Pete rattled on, "it woulda been a different story." He clenched his hard, brown fists. "So help me, Jim — I woulda spread him thin along the ground, from here to the water trough!"

"I'm sure you would," Jim muttered. He peered westward toward the ridge, which was brilliant with morning sunlight. "We'll catch up with them, Pete," he promised grimly. "Rustling horses is one thing — but forcing Joey to go with them is another."

While Pete was filling in the small details of the raid, the sheriff arrived on horseback. The two men looked at him questioningly.

"No luck yet," he announced. "I tried to get you on the phone, Jim, but found out they hadn't repaired your wire. I told them to send a lineman out. He ought to be along shortly."

"Thanks," Jim said. "You look as though you've had a hard night."

The sheriff nodded and dismounted. "Yes, but not as hard as yours, I'll bet. Is the boy okay this morning?"

"Fine," Pete said. "He's still asleep. Pore kid was plumb frazzled."

The sheriff accepted a cup of coffee and told the men about his all-night search. He and his men had had no success. While he was outlining his plans for the day, Matt Castle drove up in Sam Jackson's delivery truck.

"Morning, men," he called. "Any news?"

"Not yet," Jim replied. He got up and walked to the truck. "Mr. Castle, I want to thank you for what you did for Joey last night. If you hadn't driven along the mill creek, there's no telling what might have happened."

"That's right, Mr. Newton, but no thanks are called for. Anybody would have done what I did. My being there and finding Joey was pure chance." Castle paused to light a cigarette. "I didn't bring all that feed you ordered yesterday — figured you wouldn't need it now. But I had another order to deliver up this way, so I thought I'd drop in and ask how Joey was doing."

"He's okay," Pete said. "Sleepin' like a newborn calf."

Castle glanced toward the sheriff. "Well, sir, what are your plans for today?"

"We're going to divide into four separate groups and spiral out. If the thieves are still in the vicinity we'll find them."

"What about the area where I found Joey?" Castle asked. "Have you looked there?"

"Yep, we covered that whole section last night. Today we're hoping to find the corral before they move the horses out."

Castle looked thoughtful. "This is merely an amateur's suggestion, Sheriff, but it seems to me that if I wanted to move horses out of this valley in a hurry, I'd head toward the buttes."

"Why?"

"Well, that's pretty sparse country. And if they wanted to truck the horses out, they'd be pretty well hidden by the big rocks."

"That don't sound like such a bad idea," Pete said. "Whattaya think, Sheriff?"

The sheriff shrugged. "It's worth following up. We'll head that way first, before we spread out."

"I'll ride with you," Jim said. "I've got a big stake in this chase."

"Fine, Jim. I'll be happy to have you along."

Jim spoke to Pete. "You stay here and look after Joey."

Pete seemed about to argue, then gave in. "Wal — okay. I'd shore like to ride with ya, but till them bandits is caught I guess I oughta stick around."

Matt Castle started the motor of his truck. "I've got to make this delivery and get back to the store. Mr. Newton, if there's anything else I can do, be sure to call me."

"I'll do that, Mr. Castle. Thanks again."

Castle backed the truck around and drove away.

"Pete," Jim directed, "as soon as the phone's fixed, let the sheriff's office know. They'll be in touch with us." He unbuttoned his shirt. "Now I'd better go in and shuck these city clothes. Be right with you, Sheriff."

Jim looked in at the sleeping Joey, then hurriedly changed into his range duds. Five minutes later, he and the sheriff rode out through the gate.

When Matt Castle arrived back at the Crossroads, Sam Jackson's store was filled with people, all chattering at once about the raid on the BW. Castle greeted them cheerfully, told them that the rustlers had not been found, and walked back into the office. After he had closed and locked the door, he picked up the telephone and put in a call.

"Yeah?" said the wary voice, after the bell had rung a few times.

"Me again," Castle whispered. "All clear to talk?"

"Yep, I'm alone. But lissen, boss, the whole valley's creepin' with the sheriff's gang."

"They're nowhere near the corral, are they?"

"Nope, but I jest been up there, an' there's no sign of them trucks you said was comin'. How soon can we wheel them horses out?"

"Cool down," Castle said sternly, "you've got plenty of time."

"Sure, that's what you say. But what if the law rides up that way?"

"They won't," Castle assured his listener. "At least not for hours. That's why I called you — to tell you not to worry. I put an idea into the sheriff's head that'll take him miles out of the way this morning. They'll be riding in the opposite direction — down toward the buttes."

"But we got another problem," the voice said. "That black stallion. He's jumpin' like a grasshopper. Nobody can git near him. He's raisin' such a ruckus, we're thinkin' of puttin' a slug through his dumb head."

"Don't you dare shoot that stallion!" Castle said firmly. "I know where I can get a top price for him. More money than for all the other horses put together. You just keep him tied down, and when the trucks come, we'll handle him."

"Yeah? That's what you think."

"That's right. Now get back up there and stand guard with the others. I'll join you as soon as I can."

Castle slammed the phone down and returned to the store, smiling and ready to do business.

When Joey awoke and found himself alone in the house, he put on his clothes and went outside. The sight of Fury's empty corral brought back the sick feeling of the night before. He found Pete in the barn, repairing some stirrup leathers.

"Where's Jim?" he asked anxiously. "Did he come back?"

"He shore did — an hour ago. But he took right off agin with the sheriff."

Joey's face fell. "Without me? Gee whiz, Pete, I wanted to go with him."

"Me, too. But Jim thought it'd be better if me an' you stayed here an' kinda minded the ranch." He put the leathers aside and stood up. "Besides, Joey, huntin' hossthieves ain't no job fer a boy. Them men're gonna be ridin' hard an' fast, an' if they smoke out the rustlers there's bound to be fireworks." Pete looked down at Joey and noticed the deep puffs under his eyes. "You oughta git back to bed. You look like a spook."

"I guess I do — I had terrible dreams all night." Joey walked miserably to the barn door and looked out. "Pete, I've been thinking how we can find Fury."

"I know," Pete said sympathetically, "so've I. To tell ya the honest truth, I can't think of nothin' else. But if Jim an' the sheriff find that secret corral where

66

they took you last night, Fury'll be there. They ain't gonna do him no harm — he's too valu'ble a hoss."

"But you know how Fury is," Joey argued desperately. "He's not gonna let anybody handle him. That's why they made me ride him last night."

Pete took off his wide-brimmed hat and scratched his head. "Ya know, Joey, it's too dern bad they blindfolded you so good. If you coulda used yer eyes, ya'd have some idea 'bout where that corral is." He frowned. "Are ya shore ya din see nothin' a-tall?"

"I didn't see a thing — not once. But you know something, Pete? I *listened* real hard, the whole time I was riding."

The excitement in Joey's voice aroused Pete's curiosity. "Whattaya mean by that? What if ya did lissen hard?"

"Well, I heard the kind of ground we were going over — grass and sagebrush and shale — things like that. And I sort of memorized the order they came in, and about how long it took to go over each different place." Joey's eyes were glistening. "It's like blind people, Pete. I read once that people who can't see concentrate harder on sounds. Know what I mean? Their ears are kind of a substitute for their eyes."

Pete nodded vigorously. "Yeah, I know jest what ya mean. Once, down in the Panhandle of Texas, I met an ole, blind Injun that could guide a man anywheres jest by listenin' to the sound of his horse's hoofs on the ground. An' by echoes that bounced offa rock walls — by the wind blowin' through mesas — stuff like that."

"That's *it*, Pete!" Joey cried. "Last night I was just like that old, blind Indian!"

Pete was fascinated. "Ya mean ya heard things that ya could reckanize if ya heard 'em agin?"

"I'm sure I could! One thing I remember is going up a long rise, where Fury kicked into a bunch of little rocks. I heard them land when they hit the ground, maybe twenty feet down. Then we went across some planks that sounded hollow like a wooden bridge." He closed his eyes, reliving the experience. "Oh, and I remember something else. I heard a train. It was a diesel — I could tell by the horn."

Pete shook his head, doubtfully. "A diesel, huh? That don't help much. It could be any one of a half a dozen places. That railroad snakes fer miles along this valley, an' the track's a heck of a long ways from here."

"I know," Joey argued, "but I heard it. And right after that we went through a creek bed. There wasn't much water in it, just a trickle at the bottom — because we haven't had any rain. But Fury splashed through it, and then we climbed up the other bank." Joey turned to Pete and spoke imploringly. "Pete — can't we please ride out — just you and me? I'm almost sure we could find the place where they took Fury!"

The old foreman looked dubious. "Wal, Joey, I dunno. It might turn out to be jest a wild-goose chase."

"Sure," Joey said eagerly, "but it might work. And if we found Fury — maybe we'll find that man that sat on you and tied you up."

Pete's eyes flashed. "By jumpin' cheesecake — yer right!" He whirled and headed for the saddle rack. "C'mon, let's git goin'. I got a personal score to settle with that yella-bellied hossthief!"

Chapter 6
THE BOSS

Jim and the sheriff overtook the main group of searchers in the neighborhood of Red Mesa. The men were split into groups, riding fifty yards apart in several directions. They reported that they had found no trace of the thieves. Jim was surprised to find Mr. Barstow riding with the group. As their eyes met, Jim touched his hat and smiled. Barstow acknowledged the courtesy with a cool, unfriendly nod.

The sheriff called the men together and announced that they would leave the mesa and ride down in a body to investigate the region of the buttes. As the horses swung into line and began their journey, Jim edged his roan over beside Barstow's apron-faced bay.

"Glad to see you, Mr. Barstow," Jim said pleasantly. "I'd no idea you were riding with the sheriff's men."

Barstow kept his eyes straight ahead. "Why wouldn't I be in the party?" he asked gruffly. "It's my duty as a citizen. Besides — some of my own horses were stolen."

Jim suppressed a grin. "I know about that, and I'm sorry."

The cattleman gave Jim a side glance. He hadn't expected sympathy from the man he considered his enemy. "And I'm sorry to hear what happened at your place last night. How many did they get? Thirty-five, wasn't it?"

Jim nodded. "Thirty-five. All mustangs — and all healthy and useful." Barstow understood Jim's meaning and frowned.

"They also took Fury. That's our greatest loss."

"A magnificent stallion," Barstow admitted. "My son talks about Fury constantly."

Jim's rifle had inched up in its scabbard and he pushed it back into place. "By the way, how is David?"

"He's doing very nicely, thank you. I keep his mind occupied and see to it that he gets plenty of fresh air and recreation." A softer note crept into Barstow's voice. "I hope that by the end of the summer David will have regained his health."

"I hope so, too," Jim said sincerely. "Joey's very fond of David, and the two boys should see each other now and then."

The horses threaded their way across a gully before the men spoke again.

"I heard what happened to Joey last night," Barstow said. "It was criminal. How was he this morning?"

"Pete said he was fine. He was sleeping when I left, so I didn't get a chance to talk to him. Pete told me he felt pretty low last night, after Fury was stolen."

Barstow's eyes blazed. "If any man had abducted *my* boy the way those bandits did . . ." he slapped the walnut stock of his rifle, "I wouldn't be responsible for the outcome."

"That's the chief reason why *I'm* riding with the sheriff," Jim assured him. "Because of what they did to Joey."

Barstow twisted in his saddle and looked straight into Jim's eyes. "You mean that if you find the men, you're prepared to kill them?"

"No, I wouldn't do that," Jim said. "Not unless it was in self-defense. But I'd certainly appear against them in court if they were brought to trial."

Barstow snorted his disapproval. "That's the trouble with you, Newton, you're too softhearted. In this world there's no place for compassion."

"I disagree with you," Jim shot back. "Without tenderness, and a feeling for his fellow creatures, a man can't very easily find contentment. That means *all* creatures — four-legged as well as two."

The cattleman flushed. "I gather you still condemn me for my treatment of the mustangs."

"I certainly do, Barstow, and I'm not alone in my feelings. If you had accepted my invitation to attend the meetings at my place, you might have gained a better understanding of our position." Jim's eyes twinkled. "Who knows — you might even have been won over to the side of compassion."

Barstow's eyes were fixed on the buttes which were rising in the distance. "That's a fool statement if I ever heard one. I'll never change my mind. And if you and your committee think you can stop me by legal means, you're wasting your time. There isn't a lawmaker in the country who'll go along with you."

"I've got to disagree with you again," Jim said flatly. "Legislators in some states have already awakened to the plight of the mustangs. A number of / laws affording partial protection have been passed." As his sullen listener offered no comment, Jim warmed up to his subject. "There's a wonderful woman in Nevada — the wife of a ranch owner — who's been working for several years in the interest of mustang conservation. So far she's achieved both county and state protection, and now she's working for legislation on a national basis. In fact, this lady's congressman has agreed to introduce a protective bill into the House of Representatives in Washington, D.C." Jim noticed that Barstow had been taken aback by his recital. "You seem surprised. But surely you must have heard about all that activity."

Barstow shrugged. "Oh, I've seen something about it in various publications, but nothing will ever come of it."

"If you'll pardon my throwing your own words back at you," Jim said, "*that's* a fool statement. Animal-loving citizens all over the country are stirred up."

The cattleman looked increasingly annoyed. "I didn't come out here to receive a lecture!" he said angrily. "I came to help the sheriff find those horsethieves!" He brought his knees sharply together, and his mount leaped forward.

During the remainder of the journey to the buttes, Barstow rode at the front of the cavalcade, beside the sheriff.

As they reached the top of a long rise, Joey and Pete brought their horses to a halt and drank water from their canteens.

"Wal, Joey," Pete said, wiping his mouth, "we've been ridin' fer quite a while. Ain'tcha heard any sounds yet that ya reckanize?"

Joey sighed. "No, Pete. I've been listening hard ever since we left home, but nothing sounds the way it did last night.

"But, goldern it, this here's the third hill we've gone up, an' so far none of 'em sounded right to ya. Ya told me that Fury kicked a buncha little rocks off a hill last night, an' ya heard 'em when they hit down below." Pete scanned the ground ahead and behind. "I shore don't see no little rocks like them around here."

Joey was distressed. "I just don't know what's wrong. I was sure I could follow the trail if I listened. For a little while back there I even had my eyes shut, but it didn't do any good. Maybe I listened better when I was blindfolded." He sat still in his saddle, thinking. "Pete!" he cried suddenly. "If I was blindfolded again, maybe I could *really* find the trail!"

Pete grinned. "Mebbe so. But wouldn't ya feel

kinda silly, ridin' along blindfolded in broad daylight?"

"But you're the only one that'll see me. Come on, Pete, let's try it. You've got a handkerchief. Tie it around my eyes and lead my horse."

"Wal, okay," Pete agreed. "I'm shore of one thing — ya can't do no worse blindfolded than ya been doin'." He reached into his back pocket, took out a large, red bandana and tied it tightly around Joey's head. "There now — can ya see anythin'?"

Joey swiveled his head. "Nope — it's brighter than last night, but I can't really see anything."

"All right, off we go then." Grasping Joey's bridle, he clucked and started down the slope.

For a half hour they crisscrossed the flatland without speaking, Joey listening intently all the while for a familiar sound. A short time later, they arrived at the base of another hill.

"We got another hill in front of us," Pete called back. "What're yer orders — gen'ral?"

"Let's climb it. Maybe it's the one we're looking for."

"Okay. Up we go!"

Joey listened with all his might as the two horses made their way up the rise. When they had gone halfway to the top, his mount caught a hoof against a pile of stones. Joey's heart jumped.

"Listen!"

The stones rolled away from the crown of the hill and bounced off an outcropping of rock, twenty feet below.

"That's it!" Joey cried. "That's the sound I heard last night! This is the hill, Pete, I'm sure it is!"

"Wal, I'll be a turkey's cousin," Pete drawled, wiping his brow. "I never thought we'd make it."

"I told you we would!" Joey said triumphantly. "Let's keep on going."

At the base of the hill, around a curve of rock studded with stunted trees, they came to a small bridge. The horses cantered across, their hoofs beating out a hollow rhythm on the wooden planks.

Pete looked back at Joey. "That was a bridge."

"I know, I remember the sound." Joey's mouth, beneath the bandana, had widened into a broad grin. "Just a little way beyond here I heard the diesel. Let's look for the track."

They continued onward for another five minutes without finding a sign of the railroad.

"We ought to be near the track," Joey called. "Don't you see it anywhere?"

Pete squinted ahead through the brush. "Nope. Nary a sign of it."

"Are you sure?"

"Shore I'm shore! I ain't got *my* eyes covered up!"

Joey reached up and took off the blindfold. When his eyes had become accustomed to the brilliant light, he shaded them with his hand and stood up high in his stirrups.

"There's the track!" he whooped. "Down there — look!"

The old man's eyes followed Joey's finger. "By gum, yer right! Now yer clickin' on all cylinders."

Joey slapped his rein. "Come on! I don't need the blindfold any more. Let's find that creek bed."

76

The horses slowed down and crossed the tracks, lifting their feet daintily over the rails. Fifty yards farther on, they descended the bank of the drought-shrunken stream.

"Doggone it, Joey," Pete chuckled, "yer almost as good as that ole Injun I was tellin' ya about. You could git yerself a job as a guide — that is if ya kept yer eyes shut."

The horses splashed through the trickle of water and climbed up the opposite bank. The narrow trail beneath the trees was hard and dusty.

"Look!" Pete shouted, pointing downward. "Horseshoe tracks!"

"*Fury's* tracks!" Joey yelled joyously. "There are the marks of Fury's shoes!"

"Yer dang right they are. I put that set of shoes on him meself, jest last month."

Joey's heart was thumping. "We're getting close to that secret corral. I remember we went up just one more hill."

"Wal, this here's a pretty steep grade. Could this be it?"

Joey closed his eyes and listened to the sound of the horses' hoofs. "Yep, this is the hill all right. Oh, boy!"

"Hey, pipe down," Pete warned. "If we're gittin' so close to them bandits, we better not whoop an' holler."

Riding silently, with Pete in the lead, they reached the summit of the hill. The downward slope ahead of them was almost bare of growth. Pete reined in and beckoned.

"Look down yonder," Pete whispered.

They were peering straight down into a box canyon. At the far end was a sturdy, wooden shed, at the edge of a rope corral. Inside the corral were the Broken Wheel mustangs, standing in small groups, switching flies.

"Them's our critters," Pete muttered darkly.

"Yes!" Joey answered, straining his eyes. "And there's *Fury!*" The great, black stallion was tied securely to two trees, not far from the shed. "Come on!"

Pete darted his arm out and grasped the bridle of Joey's horse. "Hold on there! Ya wanta git yerself shot?"

"But I don't see any rustlers down there."

The old man grunted. "They're pretty close by — ya can be shore of that. We gotta be smart, Joey, an' not let 'em catch *us*."

Joey was impatient for action. "Well, let's do *something*. It won't do us any good just to sit up here and *look*."

"We're gonna do somethin', don't worry." Pete studied the surrounding hills to get his bearings. "As near as I can reckon, the Crossroads is about ten'r eleven miles southeast of here, as the crow flies. You better hightail it down there an' call the sheriff's office."

"Okay. What'll you do while I'm gone?"

"I'll keep an eye on that corral down there." Pete slapped Joey on the shoulder. "Now git goin' — an' keep that hoss in high gear all the way."

"I sure will," Joey promised. He took a last, wistful look at Fury, then mounted and started down the trail.

He had no trouble finding his way to the Crossroads.

There were no customers in Sam Jackson's store. As Joey burst through the doorway, Matt Castle was leaning over a barrel, scooping flour into ten-pound paper sacks.

"Mr. Castle!" Joey shouted. "Can I use your phone?"

The storekeeper was startled. "Joey!" he exclaimed, setting the metal scoop on the counter. "You almost scared me out of a year's growth."

"I'm sorry, Mr. Castle, but it's awful important!" Joey glanced toward the office in the rear of the store. "I've got to use your phone — *please!*"

Castle grinned. "Okay, Joey. But what're you so worked up about?"

"The rustlers! Pete and I found them! I've got to call the sheriff's office!"

The man's face turned white. "Are you sure you found the rustlers? Where?"

Joey waved his hand. "Way out there on the other side of the railroad. They're holed up in a box canyon."

Castle grabbed Joey's arm. His eyes had turned steel hard. "Did they see you?"

"No, sir, they didn't. We didn't see them, either, but we saw Fury and our other horses." Joey yanked his arm away. "We've got to hurry! Please let me call."

"Wait! Where's Pete?"

"On top of the hill. He's standing guard till I get back."

"Good! He was smart to wait." Castle ripped off his apron and started back toward the telephone. Joey was right at his heels as they reached the office doorway. Castle turned quickly. "Tell you what, Joey. *I'll* call the sheriff's office. You go to the barn and saddle my horse." He lifted the receiver.

"You going to ride back with me?" Joey asked.

"Yes. We're probably closer to that canyon than the sheriff is, so maybe I can help Pete. Now go on — hurry!"

"Okay, Mr. Castle, I'll get your horse ready."

Joey ran out through the store and leaped down the porch steps. As soon as he had disappeared, Castle carefully returned the telephone to its base. From the bottom drawer of the desk he took out a gun and placed it in his pocket.

When Pete heard the sound of horses coming up the trail, he ducked out of sight behind a tree. In a moment, Joey and Matt Castle appeared. Their horses were heaving and soapy with foam. Pete came out from hiding.

"Joey," he whispered, "did ya call the sheriff?"

Before Joey could answer, Castle spoke up. "Yes, either the sheriff or his deputies are on the way." He glanced at his watch. "They should be here shortly." He dismounted and walked with Pete to the edge of the hill. "Where's this corral Joey told me about?"

Pete pointed. "Right down there, Mr. Castle."

The storekeeper whistled in surprise. "So that's where they've been hiding. No wonder they're so hard to find."

Joey came up behind them and pointed. "There's Fury — see him? He's tied to those trees near the shed."

Castle nodded and turned to Pete. "Have you seen any men down there?"

"Yep, I seen three of 'em."

Castle frowned. "Did you recognize any of them?"

"Nope, they was too far away fer me to see their faces." He shook his head. "Goldern it, I wisht I'd thought to bring Jim's binoculars."

"They would've come in handy," Castle remarked. "Where are the men now? Did you notice where they went?"

"I shore did. I kept my eagle eye on 'em the whole time. They're all back there in that wooden shed. Sleepin', most likely, seein' as how they work nights." Pete shook his fist at the shed. "Doggone them bandits! I wisht we din hafta wait fer the sheriff."

Joey was looking down at Fury with troubled eyes. "Isn't there anything *we* can do? I'd sure like to get Fury out of there. He must think I've deserted him."

"Quit talkin' foolish," Pete said. "Fury knows better."

Castle himself seemed impatient. "Maybe we should take some kind of action. We don't want those men to slip away before the law gets here."

"What kinda action ya got in mind?" Pete asked.

"Well, you say they're inside that wooden shed.

Possibly we could slip down there and take them by surprise."

Pete snorted. "Shore — an' git ourselfs pumped fulla lead." He patted his pockets regretfully. "That's another thing I ougha brung — my forty-five. Ya can be shore them bandits is armed to the teeth."

"It looks as if I was more thoughtful than you were," Castle said.

"Whattaya mean?"

Castle drew out his gun. "I remembered to bring this."

Joey's eyes popped. "Would you have the nerve to go down there and use that?"

"Well — *I* would. I don't know anything about Pete's nerve."

The old man bristled. "I ain't afeared of no cowardly coyotes like them! If you go — I'll go!"

"So will I," Joey said.

"Ya'll do no sech thing!" Pete snapped. "Yore gonna stay right here!" He thrust his chin up toward Castle. "Wal — what the heck're we waitin' fer? Let's git goin'!" Without a further word he started down the hill."

"*Hold it!*" Castle barked sharply.

Pete jerked his head around. He was looking squarely into the barrel of the storekeeper's gun. "Hey!" he croaked in amazement. "What's the idea?"

"I'll show you," Castle answered. He raised the gun and fired twice into the air.

"Mr. Castle!" Joey cried. "You'll warn the rustlers!"

"Shut up, kid!" Castle nudged Joey toward Pete

with the muzzle of his gun. "March down the hill ahead of me!"

In the canyon, the rustlers had run from the shed and were looking around wildly, trying to locate the person who had fired the shots.

"It's okay!" Castle shouted. "It's me — Matt!"

The rustlers glanced up. "Who's that with you?" Jep called.

"Two prisoners — unarmed! We're coming down!"

"Okay, boss!" came Jep's answer.

Pete looked up at Castle with loathing and disgust. "Why, you dirty, thievin' polecat!" he muttered. "So *yore* the boss!"

Castle grinned. "That's right, old timer."

Joey was dumfounded. "But the phone! Didn't you call the sheriff?"

"No, stupid — so don't expect a rescue party." Castle pointed the gun at the back of Joey's head. "Now get going," he commanded, *"or else!"*

Chapter 7
RUSTLERS' ROUNDUP

The sheriff reined in and fired three shots into the air. It was the signal for his men to reassemble for further orders. The posse had scoured the buttes region for an hour, with no success.

"We're wasting our time down here," the sheriff announced to the circle of mounted men. "No tracks. No horsethieves. I'm open to suggestions, if anybody has any."

Jim Newton turned in his saddle and pointed back toward Indian Mountain, which was just barely visible on the shimmering horizon. "So far, nobody's checked that territory up yonder. How do you feel about giving it a try, Sheriff?"

"I'm ready to ride anywhere, Jim." He took off his white Stetson and wiped the sweatband. The skin above his hatline seemed pale in contrast to his dirt-stained face. "How about it, men? Any comments about trying that country up there?"

Barstow spoke up. "It's a long ride, Sheriff — miles beyond my ranch. And the area's wild and desolate. Searching up there would be like hunting for a needle in a haystack."

"That's true," Jim said, "but if I were looking for a place to hide a needle, I might pick that very haystack."

Barstow seemed annoyed. "If you feel so strongly about it, Newton, why didn't you suggest that we start in that direction earlier, instead of coming all the way down here to the buttes?"

The sheriff broke in before Jim could answer. "Look, I guess we're all pretty edgy, but we've got a job to do, so let's simmer down. I brought you men here at Matt Castle's suggestion. If we'd found the horsethieves in this area, Matt would be a hero. It turns out his hunch was wrong, so let's forget it and try the Indian Mountain region." He glanced up at the sun. "We've got hours before dark, so we don't have to kill ourselves or our horses hurrying." He clucked to his mount and turned north. "Come on — let's ride."

With his gun aimed at Joey's back, Matt Castle herded his two prisoners down the hill to the wooden shed. Fury jerked wildly at his double halter when Joey called his name.

"You men got that stallion well tethered?" Castle asked anxiously.

"Sure, boss," Race drawled. "Not even an elephant could git hisself loose once I tie him up."

"Don't worry, Fury!" Joey cried. "We'll get you out of here somehow!"

The three rustlers laughed. "Lissen to that dopey kid," Slim roared. "Talkin' to a horse — jest like the critter knows what he's sayin'."

"Fury understands everything I say to him!" Joey shot back.

Pete curled his lip as he recognized the group of horsethieves. "Wal, I'll be danged. I mighta knowed I'd find you three hyenas mixed up in this deal." He looked at Castle. "I wondered why you let these no-good loafers hang out in the shore."

"They're mustang-killers!" Joey said contemptuously. "I saw them with Chick Lacy, up at Mr. Barstow's ranch!"

Pete looked around the clearing. "That reminds me — where *is* Lacy? He's shore mean enough to be part of this gang."

"You talk too much, old man," Castle grunted. He motioned toward the shed with his gun. "Race, toss these two inside and lock them up."

"That'd be a pleasure," Race said. "C'mon, wise guys — inside." Grasping Pete and Joey by their shirt collars, he led them struggling through the door of the shed. "Jest in case you don't know it, you old geezer," he called in to Pete, "I'm the guy that trussed you up last night."

"Ya din hafta tell me," Pete shouted back. "A skunk smells jest the same in the light as he does in the dark!"

With an oath, Race slammed the door and fastened the wooden latch bar. When he returned to his fellow thieves, they were arguing with Matt Castle.

"So far, boss," Jep was saying, "I been followin' orders. But now I'm thinkin' about my own skin. If the old man and the kid can find this hideout, so can the law."

"Don't talk like an idiot!" Castle said hotly. "The sheriff and his men are miles from here. I sent them down to the buttes."

"So what?" Slim sneered. "When they find out we ain't at the buttes, what's to stop 'em from comin' up here?"

Jep looked anxiously up the hill. "I don't like no part of this. If they catch us down in this canyon we'll be trapped."

Race nodded. "You said it. I'm fer pullin' freight pronto."

"We're not going to abandon these horses!" Castle roared. "They're worth a lot of money."

"Not half as much as my neck's worth," said Jep. He glared at his boss accusingly. "Where's them trucks you said was gonna be here?"

Castle's eyes wavered. "They're on their way," he lied. He, too, was worried about the missing trucks. "Look, men," he continued in a more reasonable tone, "I don't blame you for your anxiety, but if we lose our heads and start to panic, our sweet little racket will be over. Now you've all trusted me so far, so why not trust me a little further? What do you say?"

The three thieves consulted each other with their eyes, but none of them spoke. Finally, Jep shrugged. "Okay, Matt, you're still boss. What's the orders?"

Castle looked relieved. "You won't regret this, so listen carefully. Each one of us has an important job to do. Race, you climb the hill and bring my horse down by the side trail. Get going!" Race took off hurriedly as Castle turned to Jep. "Jep, you and Slim ride up to Indian Mountain Lookout and see if you can spot the sheriff's party headed this way. Everybody understand?"

"Yeah, we get it," Jep said. "But what about you, boss? What're *you* gonna do?"

"I'll ride up the back trail and meet the trucks." He consulted his watch. "Let's all gather back here in — say a half hour. We'll load the horses and clear out. Got it all straight?"

"Except one thing," Slim said, pointing to Fury. "What about him? He'll be tough to handle."

Castle nodded. "I know, but with all four of us working we'll handle him — if we have to beat him senseless and drag him onto the truck. Now let's all get to work."

A short time later, after Race had returned with Castle's mount, the four horsethieves rode out of the canyon. Inside the dark shed, Pete and Joey heard the retreating hoofbeats and wondered what was happening.

"If they was on'y a peephole in this durn place," Pete muttered, "it'd shore help."

"Let's be quiet for a minute and listen," Joey said.

"Whatever you say. When it comes to listenin', yore champeen of the world."

Joey placed his ear against the wooden door. He could hear nothing outside but the stomping and snorting of the restless mustangs. The stillness inside the shed was broken only by the low drone of hornets who were keeping house on one of the roof beams.

"Hear anythin'?" the old man asked.

"Nope. I think they've all gone away."

Pete grew excited. "In that case, let's try to bust this blame door down. I'll count up to three, then let's both give it a good kick. Ready? One — two — *three!*"

Their heels met the wood with a sharp crack, but the door held fast. Pete threw his body against it, but still the latch bar on the outside didn't budge. He rubbed his bruised shoulder.

"It's no use, Joey. Whoever built this place shore done a good job of it. I guess 'bout the on'y thing we can do now is set still an' wait fer a miracle to happen."

When the sheriff's posse approached the Crossroads on the way to Indian Mountain, Jim drew up even with the leader.

"Sheriff, I'm going to drop off at the General Store for a minute and phone the Broken Wheel. I want to ask how Joey's feeling and tell Pete I probably won't be home in time for supper."

"Okay, Jim. After you've made your call, I'll check my office and tell them my plans."

When they arrived at the little settlement of stores, the sheriff told the men they could rest for a few minutes to refresh themselves and their horses. He and Jim were surprised when they went to the General Store and found it locked.

"Funny," the sheriff said. "This place hasn't been

closed in the daytime since Sam Jackson started in business."

Jim pressed his nose against the glass. "Nobody in there. But I do want to call the BW, so I'll go across to Walt's place and ask if I can use his phone. Want to come along?"

"Sure thing."

Walt, who ran a small lumberyard, engaged the sheriff in conversation while Jim put in his call. After a few minutes, Jim joined them, with a perplexed expression on his face.

"I can't understand it; they don't answer at the Broken Wheel. I checked the operator and she said the line was repaired two hours ago."

"Well, I'll phone my office," the sheriff said, "then you can try the BW again."

"Okay." Jim walked slowly from the lumberyard, deep in thought. Just outside the gate, he heard someone call his name. It was Mrs. Barton, the busy little woman who ran the dry goods store.

"Haven't you caught those horsethieves yet?" she asked.

"No, Mrs. Barton, but we're going to search up Indian Mountain way."

"Good. I hope you catch them and hang them." She glanced across at the General Store. "By the way — if you happen to meet Matt Castle on the road, tell him he'd better come back and tend to his business. Five or six customers have tried to get in since he and Joey left."

Jim scowled. "Since he and *Joey* left? What do you mean?"

"Well," Mrs. Barton explained, "I'm not one to spy on my neighbors, but I just happened to be looking out my window about an hour ago, when your Joey came racing down the road on a pinto pony. It was like he was being chased by a whole tribe of Indians on the warpath. He ran into the General Store, and a minute later he ran out again and went around back to saddle Matt Castle's horse." She paused to push a loose hairpin back into place.

"Go on," Jim said anxiously. "Then what?"

"Well, finally Matt himself came out of the store and locked the front door. Then he and Joey went riding away together. They were in a big hurry."

Jim caught her by the arm. "Which way did they go?"

Mrs. Barton pointed. "Out toward the mill creek road."

"Was Pete with them?"

She shook her head. "No, just Joey and Matt Castle."

"Thanks, Mrs. Barton." Jim turned and hurried back toward the lumberyard. He met the sheriff and told him Mrs. Barton's strange story.

"The mill creek road," the sheriff said, rubbing his jaw. "That's where the bandits left Joey last night."

Jim nodded. "I don't mind telling you I'm worried. I've no idea what happened, but you know Joey — he'd do anything in the world to get Fury back. No chance he wouldn't take."

"I know that." The sheriff's mouth was set in a straight, hard line. After he and Jim were mounted, he called the posse together. "Let's go, boys! This time, we're riding hard and fast!"

Both Pete and Joey had sore shoulders from throwing their weight against the door of the shed. Joey had not been content to wait for Pete's "miracle" to happen. Moving blindly through the darkness, he had explored every inch of the four walls, attempting to find a loose board. When he had failed, he had persuaded Pete to try once again to break the door down.

"Goldern it," Pete groaned finally, "it's no use. It's gonna take somethin' a lot stronger than the two of us to bust this door down."

"I guess you're right," Joey said miserably. "If we only had an ax or something." He drew a sharp breath. "Hey, wait a second!"

"Huh?"

"Fury! Fury can do it!"

"Sure he can," said Pete. "But he's all tied up."

"I know, but for me — maybe he can break away!" Joey made a megaphone of his hands and shouted. "Fury! Fury — it's me — Joey! Fury! Can you hear me?" From the corral came Fury's unmistakable neigh. "He heard me!" Joey cried delightedly. "Fury — come on! Get us out of here!"

In the corral, Fury whinnied and threw his body backward. Although the ropes hampered his movements cruelly, he disregarded the pain, sensing that his young master was in trouble and needed him. Again he heard Joey's cry, and again he struggled to break away, but the ropes were new and strong. In a rage, he tugged and strained, with his forelegs dug deeply into the ground. Finally, with a last tremendous effort, he hurled his great weight backward, and the ropes snapped at the loops. His momentum almost threw him to the ground on his rump, but he recovered himself and darted toward the sound of Joey's shrill voice. He leaped the corral rope with ease and came to a stop just outside the shed.

Pete and Joey heard the stallion's hoof pawing the door. "Good boy, Fury!" Joey shouted. "Now open the door! Come on, Fury, open it — the way you open your stall!"

Fury raised his hoof again, uncertain as to what action to take. As Joey and Pete pounded on the door, the stallion saw the wooden latch bar vibrate, and remembered the trick he had taught himself in his stall at the Broken Wheel. Lowering his head, he rolled his lips back and gingerly seized the bar between his teeth. Slowly, carefully, he raised it and took a step to his right. The heavy bar slid horizontally, until it passed its center of gravity and fell to the ground.

Pete and Joey pushed the door open and came whooping into the daylight. "Atta boy, Fury!" Joey cried. "You're wonderful!"

"Danged if you ain't!" Pete shouted. "I reckon you rate a whole ton of oats." He looked around anxiously for a sign of the rustlers. "C'mon, Joey," he directed. "We gotta light outa here fast." He glanced into the corral. "Them mustangs ain't manbroke yet, so I reckon we gotta ride Fury. Ya think he'll let us both on his back?"

"Sure, Pete, if I tell him it's okay." Joey grasped Fury by the mane. "Hold on, boy — Pete and I are both coming aboard." He vaulted to Fury's bare back, and leaned down to give Pete a hand. The old man threw his right leg over the broad rump, settled down and wrapped his arms around Joey's waist.

"All set," Pete wheezed. "Let's git goin'."

At Joey's command, Fury sprang forward through the open end of the box canyon. The trail ran through a grove of dwarfed cedars, then another trail crossed it at right angles. As Fury dashed past the intersection, Pete glanced quickly to his left and to his right. Joey heard a gasp, close to his ear.

"What's the matter, Pete?"

"Bad news. Them bandits're comin' down the trail from both sides."

"Do you think they saw us?"

"Either they seen us, or they're all blind as bats."

"Come on, Fury!" Joey cried. "Faster!"

Fury quickened his stride with enthusiasm. Having been tied up for half a day, he relished the opportunity to run. As the riders emerged from the trees, the vast range opened up before them. Fury gave a joyous whinny. The smooth, flat ground felt good beneath his pounding hoofs.

Pete turned his head and looked back. "Holy Hannah!"

"What is it?" Joey asked.

"They're comin' after us!"

"How many of them?"

"Three — Jep, Slim an' Castle. Uh-oh — now there's four! That Race feller sees 'em an' is joinin' up!"

Joey grimaced. "If we can only make the mill creek road — maybe we'll meet somebody!" He leaned forward. "Come on, Fury!" he yelled. "Pour it on!"

Fury swiveled his ears back and added a little extra speed. His long mane and tail streamed darkly in the wind. Under the burning sun, his body glistened with sweat. Two hundred yards behind, the rustlers continued to close the gap, little by little. Pete lost sight of them for a moment in a boiling cloud of dust, but as they emerged into clean air he knew with a sinking heart how the race would end.

"How're we doing?" Joey called.

"I hate to tell ya, but they're gainin' on us."

Joey clenched his teeth. "They can't! They *mustn't!*"

Fury thundered around an outcropping of high rocks, and the view for miles ahead was unbroken.

"There's the road!" Joey cried. "The mill creek road!" Pete's arms felt Joey's body stiffen. "And *riders!* Look, Pete — a whole bunch of riders!"

"Glory be!" Pete yelled. "Aim straight at 'em!"

Joey squinted into the sun. "It's the sheriff! I'd know that white hat anywhere!"

"Me, too!" Pete shouted happily. "Ya — *hoo!* It's jest like meetin' the U.S. Marines!"

"Jim's there, too! Look!" Joey sucked in a lungful of air and shrieked at the top of his voice. "Jim! Jim!"

The sheriff's party had spotted them and wheeled in their direction. Jim waved and called Joey's name. As the pursuing rustlers rounded the rock formation and saw the posse approaching, they came to an abrupt stop and turned their horses in the opposite direction.

Jim and the sheriff, now way out ahead of the posse, slowed down as they came abreast of Fury.

"Are you all right?" Jim cried.

"Yes," Joey called excitedly. "It's the rustlers! Matt Castle's their boss!"

"Matt Castle?" said the amazed sheriff. "With the rustlers?"

"Yeah," Pete answered. "He's chief skunk."

Jim and the sheriff spurred their horses in pursuit of the bandits. The other members of the posse swept by in a thunder of hoofs.

Pete slapped Joey on the shoulder. "Turn Fury around! Come on! I don't wanta miss any of the fun, goldern it!"

"Neither do I!" Joey urged Fury into an about-face and set out eagerly after the sheriff's men.

Far ahead, the rustlers drew their pistols and fired aimlessly. Jim and the sheriff slipped their rifles from their saddle scabbards and returned the fire. Instantly, Jep and Slim reined in and threw their hands up. Four members of the posse encircled them and took them into custody.

As Castle and Race entered the grove of cedars, Race looked back and raised his arm to fire. Before he could pull the trigger, a low-hanging bough struck him in the back of the neck and swept him from his horse. The sheriff dismounted and snapped a pair of handcuffs on his wrists.

Farther along the trail, Jim was closing the distance between himself and Castle. As Castle reached the intersecting trail, he turned and fired three times. Jim bent low over the neck of his horse as the slugs screamed over his head. The gap between the two men grew shorter, and when Jim was only ten yards from his quarry, Castle aimed his gun directly at Jim's head and pulled the trigger. It clicked sharply against the empty shell-casing. He looked at his gun in disgust and flung it back at Jim. The rustler's action had slowed his horse, and as Jim caught up with him, Castle leaped from his saddle, stumbled momentarily, and ran into the woods. Jim sprinted after the fleeing man. As Jim approached, Castle swung around and kicked out viciously. Jim grabbed the heavy boot in both hands, gave a mighty heave, and Castle turned a complete backward somersault. Castle clawed the ground, and as he rose on one knee his fingers closed around a jagged rock. Staggering to his feet, he drew his arm back and flung the rock at Jim's face. Jim sidestepped the missile and delivered a blow with the heel of his hand, full force, with the weight of his body behind it. As the hand met Castle's chin, his head snapped back and he fell limply to the ground.

When the sheriff rode up, with several of his men, Jim was standing over his fallen adversary. He pointed to Castle, who was sitting up, with surrender written on his dazed face.

"He's all yours," Jim said drily.

The sheriff nodded. "Thanks, Jim." He motioned to his men. "Take him back to the others. We'll be right with you."

Jim looked down the trail. "What happened to Joey and Pete?"

The sheriff grinned. "Joey's back there making a big fuss over Fury, but that foreman of yours — he's a problem."

Jim frowned. "Pete, a problem? What do you mean?"

"When he caught up to Race, he wanted to sock him in the jaw. It took three of my men to hold him down."

Jim threw his head back and roared. "Poor Pete. He'll never forgive you for not letting him take just one poke at the man who jumped him last night and tied him up."

Two hours later, Jim, Joey, and Pete drove their extra saddle horse and the herd of stolen mustangs into the corral at the Broken Wheel. After Joey had cleaned and curried Fury, he gave him an extra pail of oats.

"Thanks, Fury," he said softly. "Thanks for everything."

The stallion whinnied and nuzzled Joey's cheek.

Chapter 8
THE TEN-DOLLAR BILL

After a good night's sleep, Pete had gotten over his anger. In the morning he apologized to Jim and Joey for having acted so childishly, and to make it up to them he cooked a breakfast that would have done credit to the chef of an expensive restaurant. After he and Joey had finished "manicurin' the goldern dishes" — Pete's term for washing and drying — they went outside to begin their regular ranch chores. They found Jim standing in front of the porch, looking up at the sky. Although it was only seven o'clock, the temperature was already in the nineties.

"Gosh-a-mighty," Pete muttered. "If the sun keeps blazin' down like this, the whole dang state'll jest natcherly dry up an' blow away."

Jim shook his head. "Since we built this ranch we've never had such a long spell without rain. How're the pumps doing, Pete?"

"Oh, we're gittin' a little trickle outa them — jest about enough to fill the troughs. But if they go dry I reckon we'll hafta start haulin' water." He winced at the thought. "Jest thinkin' about carryin' them metal drums makes my back ache."

"We might be forced to do it though," Jim said, "if the drought gets any worse."

While they were discussing the doubtful possibility of rain, the sheriff's car drove through the ranch gate. The drought was forgotten momentarily, as they gathered around the car to hear the latest news on the captured rustlers. The sheriff had questioned the prisoners in their cells until long past midnight. As far as he could gather, Jep, Slim, and Race had no previous criminal records, but Matt Castle had confessed to having served several prison terms for swindling ranchers in other states. Judge Morris had given the sheriff a warrant to search the General Store, and two deputies were spending the morning there, going over the place with a fine-toothed comb.

"What about Chick Lacy?" Joey asked. "I'll bet he was mixed up in that rustling too, only we didn't catch him at it."

"Joey!" Jim said in a severe tone. "It isn't fair to accuse a man of wrongdoing just because you don't like him."

"I know, Jim, but Chick Lacy worked with Jep and Slim and Race all the time while they were catching the mustangs."

"What does that prove? Lacy might have associated with those men, but that doesn't make him guilty of their crime. If you want to be a decent citizen, you've got to learn not to make hotheaded accusations."

Joey was shamefaced. "I'm sorry, Jim. I guess I did say that just because I hate Chick for what he's doing to the wild horses."

"All right, Joey," Jim said more quietly, "let's forget it. I hope you've learned a lesson."

The sheriff had been listening with interest. "Jim's right, son; that's a valuable lesson we all have to learn sooner or later."

Pete spoke up, sheepishly. "I got a confession to make, fellas. I felt the same way as Joey about that Chick Lacy. But now I see I oughtn't to of suspected him."

"Well, I'll tell you something," the sheriff said. "As a peace officer it was my duty to investigate the possibility of Lacy's being mixed up in the horse-stealing. But when I questioned the rustlers about him, all four of them said that Chick had nothing to do with it. Of course, they might have been lying for some reason, so I'm going to question Chick personally as soon as I get to Barstow's."

"You goin' up there now?" Pete asked.

"Yes, I want to look through the belongings of those three bandits who worked for Barstow. I may find some useful evidence, although I doubt it. I phoned Barstow awhile ago and asked his permission to look around his bunkhouse. He wasn't very happy about giving it, but he finally broke down and gave me an okay." The sheriff turned to Jim. "I'd like you to drive up with me. I'll need a witness while I'm searching the bedrolls and gear. How about it, Jim, will you do me that service?"

"Of course, if you need me." He shook his head doubtfully. "But since Barstow and I are on opposite sides of the mustang question, I'm not exactly welcome up there."

"I'd like you to come along anyway. This morning's business has to do with rustlers, not mustangs." The sheriff opened the door of his car. "Come around and hop in."

"May I go with you, Sheriff?" Joey asked eagerly.

"Sure, why not?"

"Hold on now," Jim warned. "You're no more welcome at Barstow's than I am."

"I know, Jim, but I want to see David."

Jim nodded. "Okay, Joey, get in. I suppose he'd be happy to see a friend."

As they drove northward across the arid range, they discussed the drought. The sheriff told them that Bill Gibson, the firewarden, was closing the entire valley to hunters and picnickers. The natural growth on the range and in the hills had become so dry that one tiny spark or campfire could destroy thousands of acres of priceless timberland. Joey launched into a long description of his weekly patrols on fire duty, and while he was still talking they drove through the gate of the Barstow ranch.

Jim had been right. Barstow soon made it clear that he and Joey were not welcome. David, on the other hand, was delighted at seeing Joey again. While the three men were in the bunkhouse inspecting the rustlers' possessions, the boys perched themselves on the fence of the main corral. David was eager to hear about Joey's adventure with the rustlers, and Joey told him the whole story. When it was over, David said he wanted to see Fury again, and Joey invited him to come down to the Broken Wheel whenever he felt like it.

"Gosh," David said wistfully. "It must be wonderful to be allowed to go out whenever you feel like it and ride around on Fury the way you do." He glanced toward the bunkhouse. "I wish my dad wasn't so strict with me all the time."

"Well," Joey said tactfully, "your dad does take you out on hunting and fishing trips. That's pretty good fun, isn't it?"

David looked away. "Yes, I guess so but — well — maybe after school starts it'll be different." He sighed. "Dad's going to take me on a hunting trip soon. I — I guess that'll be fun."

"Wait a minute," Joey said. "You can't go on a hunting trip — not till the weather breaks."

"Why not?"

"The firewarden's closed the valley on account of the drought."

Joey explained about the danger of fire during the dry spell, and outlined his own duties as a Junior Forest Ranger. David listened with intense interest and understood.

"I'm glad you told me all about it, Joey. It'd be awful if Dad and I started a forest fire by accident. I'll tell him you said we can't go hunting until the dry spell's over."

"Hey, wait!" Joey said in alarm. "Don't tell him *I*

said so. Just tell him the firewarden said so. That way, I think he'll understand better."

"Yes," David agreed, "I see what you mean." He heard voices and glanced up the road. "Here they come now. I wonder if they found anything in the bunkhouse."

As the three men approached the corral, Mr. Barstow's voice could be heard above the others. As usual, the cattleman was anything but calm.

"Sheriff," the boys heard him saying, "I suppose you've done what you call your duty. Now that you've searched my bunkhouse without finding anything, I've no doubt that next you'll want to search my ranch house."

"No, Mr. Barstow," the sheriff said in a calm, even voice, "I don't want to do any such thing. What makes you think I'd want to invade your privacy?"

"Well, since those three scoundrels were on my payroll, I'm sure you suspect me of harboring criminals knowingly."

"Look," the sheriff argued patiently, "you've misunderstood my reason for coming up here. You may be a difficult man at times, but everyone knows you're honest."

"Thank you," Barstow said sarcastically. "But if you're so convinced of my honesty, why did you bring Jim Newton with you?"

"I told you," the sheriff answered testily. "I needed an outside witness while I was searching."

"But why Newton? Why not a hundred other men?"

"I'll tell you later," the sheriff said. "Here comes a man I want to talk to — Chick Lacy."

All heads turned as Lacy came ambling down the road from the north pasture. In his dirty jeans and stained black shirt he resembled a hobo who had been on the road for weeks.

"Lacy!" the sheriff called. "Would you come over here, please?"

Lacy shuffled with exasperating slowness toward the group at the fence, his boots kicking up small swirls of dust. As always, he was chewing a matchstick. "Wal, fry my hide," he drawled arrogantly, as he looked at the sheriff. "I'll be a prairie dog's cousin if it ain't the man with the star."

"Lacy," the sheriff said flatly, "I'd like to ask you a few questions."

Lacy ran his fingers through his black hair and turned his sleepy eyes on Barstow. "How about it, boss? This little confab okay with you?"

"Yes, get on with it," Barstow snapped impatiently. "The sooner these men leave, the sooner I can get back to work."

Chick glanced at Jim and Joey. "I see the little pals of the noble mustang are here, too. Am I gonna git some lessons on how to drive a jeep — or mebbe how to put out fires?"

"Whenever you're ready to learn," Jim said directly, "Joey and I are ready to teach."

"Come on, come on!" Barstow urged. "Get it over with!"

Chick draped his long arm over the top rail of the fence. "Okay, Sheriff, you heard the man, so git on with it."

"I want to ask you about Jep, Slim, and Race," the sheriff began.

"Yeah, that's what I figgered."

"What do you know about them?"

"I know they're in jail, Sheriff — that is, unless they busted out when you wasn't lookin'."

"They're in jail all right, and they're going to stand trial. What else do you know about them?"

Lacy shrugged. "Nothin'."

"But you worked with them often enough, roping mustangs from your jeep. Didn't you ever hear them talking about rustling horses for Matt Castle?"

"Nope." Chick looked at Jim and chuckled derisively. "We was always too busy catchin' wild horses for Mr. Barstow."

"If you did know they were rustling, you could be prosecuted for not reporting them to me. I suppose you know that."

"Yep, I know that." Chick's heavy eyelids flickered. "Lissen, Mr. Law — if Jep or Slim or Race told ya I was mixed up in their rustlin', they was lyin'. I didn't know nothin' about it." He wiped his nose on his greasy sleeve. "*Did* they say I was mixed up in it?"

"No, Lacy, they didn't."

Chick seemed relieved. "Okay then — I guess that ends this here third degree." He dropped his attitude of lazy cynicism and spoke angrily to Jim. "Newton, I reckon I got *you* to thank fer gittin' the sheriff on my neck!"

"You're wrong, Lacy," Jim said earnestly. "I never mentioned your name in connection with this rustling."

"No? Then it musta been this brat of yores!" He

glared at Joey, then turned and slouched up the road. "If ya want me, boss," he called back, "I'll be in the bunkhouse."

"Now that that's settled," Barstow said sternly, "I'll ask you three to get off my ranch."

"Before we go," the sheriff said, "I want you to know that coming up here was my own idea. I asked Jim to come with me because he was directly concerned with the capture of the rustling gang."

"And he'd like nothing better than to give me trouble!" The cattleman's face was flushed with anger. "Newton bears a grudge against me because I'm ridding the range of his precious mustangs!"

"That's not true, Barstow!" Jim shot back. "I bear no grudge against you. I'm simply trying as a humane person to stop your cruelty to the wild horses. And now that three of your hired torturers have been arrested, this would be a good time for you to bring the whole thing to an end."

Barstow was shaking. "I'm going to continue until the mustangs are exterminated! In fact, I've already hired three new men to work with Chick Lacy! They start tomorrow morning." He turned to his son and lowered his voice. "Come on, David, it's too hot for you out here. I'll take you to the house."

David hesitated. "Dad — Joey asked me to come down to the Broken Wheel and see Fury. May I go — please?"

"No, son," his father answered firmly, "you may not." He saw the disappointment in the boy's face, and spoke more sympathetically. "You've got to understand why I forbid it, David. Please try."

"We'll be going now, Mr. Barstow," the sheriff said. "We're sorry to have troubled you."

Barstow stood silent as the three visitors climbed into the car.

"So long, David," Joey called. "See you when school starts."

David raised his hand and waved it listlessly. The sheriff swung the car around the circle and drove away. Nothing had been gained by the visit but the further hostility of Barstow and Chick Lacy.

"Well, Sheriff," Jim said, as they sped down the valley, "what's your professional opinion of Chick Lacy?"

The sheriff thought for a moment before answering. "I've met his kind before, Jim. He pictures himself as a 'strong, silent man.' For some reason that's the kind of character he admires. With his 'to-heck-with-everything' attitude he'd like the world to believe that he doesn't give a hoot about anything; but that attitude is strictly phony and only skin deep. That bored expression he wears is only a mask to hide his real, angry feelings. It drops right off the minute something bugs him. You saw it drop when he accused you of getting me on his neck."

"I sure did," Jim said.

"We saw it drop once before, too," Joey added. "The day he got sore at me for warning him about throwing lighted cigarettes in the grass. He gave me a crack on the head, and Fury butted him in the seat of his pants."

The sheriff chuckled. "I'd like to have seen that."

"It was funny at the time," Jim said seriously,

"but I'm afraid both Joey and Fury made an enemy that day."

"You're right," the sheriff agreed. "Lacy's mean and cruel, and he'll bear watching. However, I'm fairly sure that he had no part in the rustling. The four men now in jail denied that he was involved and I feel inclined to believe them. Facing prison terms anyway, they'd have no reason to say Lacy was innocent if he wasn't. They'd want him to go to jail, too."

When the car arrived at the BW, the sheriff dropped off Jim and Joey and drove back to town. He was impatient to learn what, if anything, his two deputies had turned up in their search of the General Store.

That evening, when *The Valley Mirror* printed an extra edition, the front page story about what the deputies had turned up caused a sensation. Among the store's cash receipts was a ten-dollar bill which the bank identified as part of the loot taken the previous winter in the robbery of a Federal Reserve Bank in Helena, Montana. Eighty thousand dollars had been stolen, in tens, twenties and hundreds. Fortunately, the robbed bank had recorded the serial numbers of the missing currency and had issued a confidential warning to banks throughout the country to be on the lookout for any of the stolen bills. The ten-dollar note found in the General Store was the first one to make an appearance.

According to the newspaper story, the bank theft in Helena had been committed by two men, one of whom had been killed while attempting to escape.

His partner had made a clean getaway with the stolen money. The bank teller who had handed over the loot had given an incomplete description of the escaped robber. He could remember only that the man wore a brown leather jacket and had hair of a light color.

When the police technicians dusted the counter of the teller's cage for fingerprints, they found a full set put there by a man's right hand. The prints matched a set already in the identification files, so the police knew the name of the man they would have to find. The name was not announced to the public, but ever since the robbery the criminal had been sought by law enforcement agencies throughout the country.

Matt Castle was not the man for whom the police had been searching. The fact that he had not even been an outside accomplice in the bank robbery was proven when the records showed that he had been serving a term in a Tucson jail when the crime was committed. The police were then forced to assume that the ten-dollar bill had been given to Castle as payment for goods purchased at the store. When questioned, Castle said logically that it was impossible for him to recall which customer had given him the bill. His statement was accepted, because many other bank notes of the same denomination were found among his cash receipts.

When asked by a reporter from *The Valley Mirror* why the bank robber had so far spent only ten dollars of his eighty-thousand-dollar haul, the police chief advanced his theory that the man had spent it as a test. The fugitive, the chief surmised, was getting impatient after seven months of holding a small fortune, and wanted to see whether he could start spending his "hot" money without its being recognized.

The drama of the ten-dollar bill, following so closely on the heels of the rustling incident, provided the valley dwellers with unaccustomed excitement. Those who had tens or twenties in their wallets took them out and studied them curiously, fascinated by the thought that the bills might be part of the bank loot.

That night, at the Broken Wheel Ranch, Pete examined three ten-dollar bills which he had been hiding in an old pair of boots against a rainy day.

"Wal, I'll be danged," he said to Joey in surprise. "This's the first time in my whole life I ever reelized that Alex Hamilton's picture was on the front of a sawbuck."

"There were some hundred-dollar bills in that bank loot, too," Joey said. "Show me one, Pete, and let's see whose picture's on it."

Pete scowled. "Have you gone plumb loony? I ain't never even seen a hundred-dollar bill in my life, an' I don't reckon I ever will."

In various parts of the valley, ranchers' wives refused to retire for the night until all the doors and windows had been closed and bolted. A desperate criminal had paid a visit to the vicinity, and for all they knew he was still among them, crouching in the darkness, waiting to murder them in their beds and make off with their money.

Pete was no different from the ranchers' wives. Before he turned out the light in his bedroom he tucked his three ten-dollar bills under his pillow, right next to his trusty shootin' iron.

Chapter 9
RED BAKER

Several days after the discovery of the ten-dollar bill, a stranger appeared at the Broken Wheel Ranch. As his ramshackled jalopy turned through the gate and chugged slowly and noisily up the road past the corrals, Fury threw his ears forward and danced nervously alongside the fence.

The young man at the wheel leaned out over the dented door and waved at the stallion in a friendly manner. "Hi there, handsome," he called. "Sorry to be making so much racket, but I can't help it. This broken-down heap of mine is sick, sick, sick."

Fury raised his head and made a sound that was somewhere between a startled whinny and a disapproving neigh. The visitor laughed and continued on to the barn, where Jim, Pete, and Joey were watching his rackety approach with disbelief written on their faces. He stopped the car and turned off the motor. It wheezed pathetically, coughed several times, and died.

The newcomer grinned at the welcoming party. "Good morning," he called cheerfully. "I can see by your faces that you never thought my limousine could make it up your little hill. That black horse down there didn't think so, either. When I whizzed by him at my customary eleven miles per hour he made a peculiar sound. I'm not sure, but I think he gave me a horselaugh."

"That's Fury," Joey said. "I don't think he's ever seen a jalop — I mean a car like yours."

"Nobody has," the young man admitted. "But Bessie brought me all the way from Chicago, believe it or not. If you'll wipe the dust off her license plates, you'll see the word, Illinois." He grinned boyishly. "Well, now that you know my car's name, I'd better tell you mine. It's Red Baker."

Jim came forward and introduced himself and the others.

"I'm certainly glad to meet some genuine westerners," the visitor said. "May I get out and stretch my legs?"

"You sure may," Jim answered pleasantly.

Red Baker opened the squeaky door of his car and stepped out. From head to foot he was dressed like a movie cowboy, with high-heeled boots, blue jeans, and a green silk shirt. Around his neck was a yellow silk handkerchief. A ten-gallon hat lay on the front seat.

Red was about twenty-nine years of age, a trifle under six feet in height, and built like an athlete. A lock of unruly hair, a shade lighter than auburn, hung down across his forehead. The most striking features of his face were his broad, smiling mouth and his large eyes, which were blue and friendly.

Pete studied Red's costume with open disapproval. "That's some git-up yer wearin'," he remarked drily. "You a broncbuster?"

Red chuckled. "*Me* — a broncbuster? No, Pete, I'm a professional entertainer—at least that's what I like to think I am." He pointed to a guitar case, wedged in between two battered valises on Bessie's back seat. "I'm what they call in show business a 'singing cowboy.' "

"Oh, one-a them," Pete said distastefully.

Joey was entranced. "Have you acted in any western movies or TV shows?"

"Not yet, Joey," Red answered, rather wistfully. "I've sung around in small nightclubs and places like that, but I've never done any real acting. That's why I happen to be out here, so far west of Chicago. I'm on my way to Hollywood, hoping to break into pictures." He pushed the lock of hair up from his forehead. "The trouble is, I ran out of money a few days ago, and since then I've been driving Bessie around your valley, trying to find a few days' work."

"Have you had any luck?" Jim inquired.

"Not so far, Mr. Newton."

"Why not call me Jim?"

"Thanks, Jim, I will." Red glanced about the ranch with satisfaction. "This is a fine setup you've got here. Any chance of a little work for a week or so?" He grinned. "My mind isn't so sensational, but I've got a strong back."

"You certainly look like a healthy specimen," Jim said. "Let me think."

Joey looked up at Jim, hopefully. He liked Red Baker and was enthralled by the idea of his being a professional entertainer, perhaps even a future movie star.

Jim turned to Pete. "What do you think? Is there anything Red can do to help us out temporarily?"

Pete rubbed the stubble on his chin. "Wal, I dunno," he said doubtfully. "Red told us hisself he's no ranch hand, in spite of his fancy cowboy git-up. I dunno what a feller like him could do around here."

"I know what," Joey said eagerly. "Red could help us haul water from the lake."

Pete's eyes lit up. The idea of having a helper in filling and carrying the heavy steel drums appealed to him. "Yeah," he agreed almost cheerfully, "that's one job I reckon he could do real good."

"Okay, Red," Jim decided, "you're hired for a week — maybe longer if the drought keeps up."

Red was delighted. "Thanks a lot, Jim. I appreciate it more than I can say."

Pete grunted. "Mebbe you won't appreciate it so much after a day of that backbustin' work."

"You can make yourself comfortable in the bunkhouse," Jim said. "Joey, show Red where he can park Bessie and stow his things. Red, you'll take your meals with us. Lunch will be ready shortly."

Later, as the four sat around the table eating their noonday meal, Red Baker told them about his work

116

as a singing cowboy entertainer. Both Joey and Jim found his account interesting, and asked numerous questions. Pete, on the other hand, listened in grim silence, keeping his head down but peering at Red from time to time from beneath his bushy eyebrows. When he had sopped up the last drop of gravy from his plate with a piece of bread, he wiped his fingers and pointed at Red.

"Look, young fella," he said almost belligerently, "if you figger on bein' one-a them movie or TV cowboys, you ain't got a chancet."

"Haven't I?" Red asked in surprise. "Why do you say that?"

"Wal, fer one thing, you ain't got no western drawl. Actors in them western movies don't talk like they jest got outa college, like you do — leastways, none that I ever seen."

Red sat back and thrust his thumbs into his belt. "Wal now, pardner," he said with a thick western twang, "I shore think you got a good argyment there. But when I'm a-hootin' an' a-hollerin' with my ole *git*-tar, I kin drawl the owls down outa the trees."

Joey laughed at the amazed expression on Pete's face. "That was wonderful, Red," he said gleefully. "You sounded exactly like Pete."

Red reached out and shook Joey's hand. "Thanks for the compliment. There's nothing I like better than an appreciative audience."

"You can really turn that accent on and off, can't you?" Jim said.

Red nodded. "Yes, I suppose I'm not too bad at

it. At least I've managed to fool a few nightclub audiences."

"But a western drawl ain't enough," Pete argued. "If ya ever land in the movies, ya'll be called on to ride an' rope an' shoot. Can ya do any-a them things?"

"No, Pete," Red admitted, "that drawl is my only cowboy talent. But while I'm working here at the ranch, maybe I can learn some of those skills you mentioned."

"I'll teach you," Joey said earnestly. "When I first came to the ranch I couldn't do any of those things, either. But now I'm pretty good at all of them."

"I'll bet you are," Red said. "I'll tell you what, Joey — if you teach me to ride and rope and shoot, I'll teach you how to play a tune on the guitar."

Joey was pleased. "Boy, that'd be great!" He jumped up from the table. "Come on, Red let's get your guitar and you can start right now."

"Hold on, Joey," Jim said. "We hired Red Baker to haul water, not to give music lessons. He'll get his guitar out tonight, after the work's done. Now suppose you take Red out behind the barn and show him where we've stacked the water drums. And get him a set of work clothes. Pete and I will be out after a bit to help you. It's a big job and we've all got to pitch in."

After Joey and Red had left the house, Pete seemed fretful and peevish.

"What's bugging you?" Jim asked.

"You know goldern well what's buggin' me," the old man snapped. "It's that Red Baker, all dressed

118

up in them dude cowboy duds. I don't cotton to fake cowboys — never did."

Jim was amused. "Don't let his costume worry you, Pete. He seems like a nice enough young fellow, and Joey seems pleased to have him around. And don't forget — if Red Baker *should* make good in Hollywood, you'll be proud to tell people you knew him when."

"Mebbe," Pete muttered. "First let's see if he can make good handlin' them steel water drums."

"I'll bet you a pair of boots he'll do a good job," Jim said.

Pete made a face. "Yeah — we'll see."

In the bunkhouse, Joey gave Red Baker a workshirt and a pair of faded Levis. While Red was changing, Joey examined his guitar with great interest, and asked a torrent of questions.

"Hey, Red, when you're doing your act what kind of songs do you sing?"

"Oh, all kinds of western ballads. Many of the old favorites and sometimes new ones that I compose myself."

"You mean you can make songs up?"

"Yes, it's a little talent I learned. Might come in handy if I ever get that break in pictures or TV."

"You'll get it, Red," Joey said confidently, "I know you will. And when you're a big star I'll go and see all your movies."

"Thanks for believing in me. It's good to know I have one fan, even before I start." He looked out the window while he was pulling on his Levis. "One thing I'd like to do while I'm staying here at the

Broken Wheel — that's to look around the valley and see real cowhands at work. Living in the city, I've never actually had that opportunity."

"I'll be glad to take you around," Joey said. "I know every ranch in the valley. But gosh," he added regretfully, "you can't ride a horse."

Red shrugged. "That doesn't matter. We'll drive around in Bessie, okay?"

"Sure, that'd be swell."

While they were unstacking the water drums, Joey told Red about the rustlers and the discovery of the ten-dollar bill from the bank robbery. Red said that he had heard about all the excitement while he was riding around the valley looking for work, and thought it was "just like in the movies." During the afternoon, while they were filling and hauling the water drums, Joey chattered away like a magpie. By the time the troughs were filled, Red was up to date on the facts of Joey's life at the BW, from the taming of Fury to the crusade against Mr. Barstow for his cruelty to the mustangs.

Red was curious about Chick Lacy. "I didn't get as far as the Barstow ranch," he said, "but from the description you've given me of Lacy he sounds like one of those blackhearted western villains. Is he really as bad as you've painted him?"

"I don't know much about him," Joey admitted, "except what I've told you. But he's certainly got a mean temper."

"He must have, from what you've told me." Red dampened his handkerchief in the horse trough and squeezed the water onto the back of his neck. "How long has Chick Lacy been working for Mr. Barstow, Joey?"

"Since early last month. Why?"

"Oh, I just wondered." Red picked up an empty drum and swung it with ease onto the truck. "Jim said this will probably be the last load for today, so let's get going."

Jim, who had been keeping an eye on Red Baker's work all afternoon, was pleased. Even Pete admitted to Jim privately that "fer a fake cowboy he din do a bad job."

After supper, Red brought his guitar over to the ranch house and sang a number of cowboy songs. Before long, Joey, Jim, and finally Pete himself, were singing along with Red, and the rafters rang with such old favorites as "Home on the Range," "The Cowboy's Lament," and "The Old Chisholm Trail." When Pete's voice cracked on a high note, the others laughed good-naturedly.

Pete turned crimson. "What're ya cacklin' at?" he asked angrily. "I ain't supposed to be no Caruso! I'm a mustanger — not one-a them crooners!" He glared at Red Baker and stomped off to his room.

"He'll get over it," Jim assured Red in a low voice. "Like all old cowhands, Pete's always just a little suspicious of city folks."

"I know," Red grinned. "I'm not worried." He handed the guitar to Joey. "Here you are. Time for your first lesson."

Joey wrapped his small hand around the neck of the instrument, and Red showed him how to finger a few basic chords. Joey could just about reach "C," but the "G" chord was too much of a stretch for his short fingers.

"That'll do for tonight," Red told him finally. "But before I leave the Broken Wheel I promise to have you playing a tune." He returned the guitar to its case and walked to the door. "Come out with me, Joey. Before it gets dark I want to meet that great horse of yours. I must have passed him twenty times today, but I haven't really been properly introduced."

As Joey came down the road with Red, Fury gave a whinny of welcome and pranced over to the fence of his corral.

"Fury," Joey said, "I'd like you to meet my friend Red Baker. Red, this is Fury."

"I'm delighted to meet such a great celebrity," Red said with a bow. "Joey has told me all about you, and if I had a pencil and paper I'd ask you for your autograph."

Fury thrust his muzzle over the top rail and sniffed Red's shoulder. Satisfied that Red was a good fellow to know, he brushed his cheek with his soft nose.

"See?" Joey exclaimed happily. "He likes you!"

Red was pleased at having been accepted as a friend. "I like him, too, Joey. Will he let me touch him?"

"Sure, just pat his nose."

Fury made small sounds of pleasure as Red first caressed his nose, then slid his hand up confidently and fondled his ears.

Joey seemed surprised. "Boy, Red, most people

that don't know horses are afraid to do that. They always think they'll get bitten or something."

Red drew his hand back quickly. "Really? I guess I was just too ignorant about horses to be afraid."

"Well, you'll certainly learn plenty about them while you're at the BW."

Red studied the great black stallion in admiration. "Joey," he said finally, "it must be great to ride a magnificent horse like Fury. I'll bet you're proud to be his owner."

"You said it." Joey stepped on the bottom rail of the fence and threw his arms around Fury's neck. "When those rustlers stole him I felt just awful." He planted a kiss on Fury's head, just below his ear. "But we'll never be separated again in our whole lives, will we, Fury?"

Fury made a deep, loving sound in his throat.

"Your love for each other seems to be mutual," Red said.

"It sure is." Joey stepped down from the fence. "Gosh, Red, I wish you knew how to ride a horse. If you only could, then we wouldn't have to drive around in Bessie when I show you the other ranches."

Red shook his head regretfully. "I wish I could ride, too. But then, Bessie isn't so bad, even if she does need new spark plugs."

After bidding Fury good night, Red and Joey began walking back to the house.

"Fury," Red murmured. "Fury — that wouldn't be bad at all."

"What wouldn't?" Joey asked.

"I was just thinking. Fury — that would be a good title for a song."

Joey grinned. "You mean — you'd write a song about Fury?"

"Yes, why not? A western style ballad. We might call it 'The Ballad of Fury.' "

"That'd be wonderful!" Joey said excitedly. "Are you going to write it now?"

"No, not now — I'm too tired to think straight. But I'll have it for you in a couple of days."

"Oh, boy, a song about Fury! I can hardly wait to hear it!"

Red leaned back in his rocker, completely relaxed for the first time since his arrival at the ranch. He was gazing westward toward the hills which stood like gray humps against the vivid sky of evening. "Joey," he said in a soft voice, "I wonder if you realize how lucky you are to be living out here. It's hard to believe that not too long ago this land was wilderness." He raised his arm and pointed. "You see that pass that runs up there between the two ridges?" Joey nodded. "A century ago, long wagon trains wound their way slowly through that narrow canyon, and the men who drove the oxen had no idea what they'd find on the other side. Somehow they just knew in their tired bones that somewhere out there was a new land and a new life. And that assurance gave them the courage and strength to continue onward, day after day."

Joey listened to Red's stories of the trail for a long time, and soon after darkness fell he went off to bed, to dream of broken axles, Indian raids, and covered wagons being floated across rain-swollen rivers.

A few minutes later, when Jim came out, Red was sitting alone on the porch. "I heard what you were telling Joey," Jim said. "I liked it."

Red smiled. "Oh? I had no idea you were listening."

"I couldn't help overhearing. I hope you don't mind."

"On the contrary, Jim, I'm pleased."

Jim settled down in the chair beside Red.

"Joey's a fine boy," Red said. "You should be proud to be his father."

"I'm proud, all right, but I'm not his father."

Red looked around in surprise. "You're not?"

"No, I adopted him from the Children's Home in town."

"Hm," Red said, "Joey didn't tell me that. Now *I* have something new to think about. How did it all happen? Do you mind telling me?"

"No, Red, I'd like to tell you."

Jim put his feet on the porch railing and began to talk. He had known Red Baker for only a short time, but already he felt drawn toward the man for his sensitivity and warm friendliness. Feeling certain that Red was genuinely fond of Joey, Jim spoke tenderly and at length about his own love for the boy. By the time Jim had finished, Red had learned how Joey first came to the ranch, how he had earned Fury's love and confidence, and how he had made himself an essential part of Jim's life.

Later, in the bunkhouse, Red Baker lay for a long

time in troubled wakefulness. The fact that he had knowingly deceived his new friends at the Broken Wheel, and had lied to them about the real purpose of his coming, made sleep an impossibility.

Chapter 10
"THE BALLAD OF FURY"

The continuing dry spell doubled the work at the Broken Wheel. Before the regular ranch chores could be tackled, the water troughs had to be filled, and this meant that everyone had to rise an hour earlier each morning to get the job under way. Red Baker proved to be such a great help in the water-hauling operation that Jim wondered how it could have been done without him.

Late in the afternoon of Red's third day at the BW, he and Joey set out in poor, broken-down Bessie for a tour of the neighboring ranches. Red was excited at the prospect of seeing real cowboys at work. As they clattered down past the corral, Fury ran to the fence and gave Bessie another one of his ungentlemanly horselaughs. Red braked the car and leaned out.

"Fury," he said in a tone of mock reproof, "it's high time you learned not to criticize others for their physical infirmities. Bessie may look like something the cat dragged in, but despite her ugly exterior, she's terribly sensitive. Hereafter, when she passes by your corral, I wish you'd either look the other way or keep your uncomplimentary opinions to yourself."

As if in answer to Red's reprimand, Fury rolled his lips back and repeated the raucous sound. Unable to keep a straight face any longer, Red roared with laughter.

Joey was laughing too. "Boy, Red — Fury sure told you off! That was the funniest thing I've ever seen him do."

"It was funny all right. You know, I'll bet Fury and Bessie would make a great comedy team." Red threw the car in gear, and with a great clashing and grinding, it crept slowly toward the gate. Fury gave an anxious whinny and ran alongside Bessie until he was stopped by the lower fence of his enclosure.

Joey looked back at him regretfully. "Poor Fury, he wants to come along. He can't understand why I'm leaving him."

"You can blame it all on me," Red said. "If I were a genuine cowboy, you and I would be riding horseback instead of puttering along in old Bessie." The jalopy chugged through the gate. "Which way shall we go? You call the turns."

"Let's go north," Joey suggested, pointing to his right. "There's a lot of real big ranches up that way."

As they bumped along the dirt road which cut

through the center of the valley, Joey pointed suddenly toward the crest of the ridge. "Look!" he cried angrily. "That's Mr. Barstow's bush pilot! He's after the mustangs again!"

Red looked up and saw the plane, circling low over one of the canyons. "Does that mean that there's a new jeep crew working?"

"Yes, Mr. Barstow told us he was hiring some new men to work with Chick Lacy. It's just awful, Red! When those wild horses get scared and run down onto the plateau they're going to be tortured!"

Red shook his head sympathetically. "I certainly hope Jim and his committee can put a stop to it." He glanced at Joey. "Do you think we could drive up and see that jeep crew? I'd like to watch how they operate."

Joey shook his head. "Bessie could never make it. There's no real road leading up there. Only a jeep can get through."

"Well, maybe I can see them some other time."

As they proceeded onward, Joey felt heartsick as he watched the swooping plane. When they reached the Lazy M Ranch, Red pulled him out of his depression by pointing to activity in one of the corrals.

"Look, Joey. What're those men doing?"

"Breaking broncs. You're lucky — that's just the kind of stuff you wanted to see."

They got out of the car and stood by the fence. As they watched the frisky animals being broken, Joey explained the action like an announcer at a rodeo. The bucking horses were kicking up clouds of dust. Suddenly, one of the bronc-peelers came down when he should have been going up, and went sailing through the air.

"Ouch!" Red muttered when the man hit the hardpan. "That even hurt *me*."

"Me, too," Joey said. "Think you'll ever learn to do that?"

"Gosh, I don't know. If that's what a cowboy actor has to do, maybe I ought to give up the whole idea and be a used-car salesman."

They watched the free show for a while longer, then returned to Bessie and drove farther up the road to the Triple X layout, where a group of men were hazing steer into the stockpens. After they had watched this action a while, Joey glanced at the sun and told Red it was time they were heading back to the Broken Wheel.

"Have we a few minutes to take a quick look at the Barstow ranch?" Red asked.

"Why?"

"After all you've told me about it, I'm curious to see it."

Joey shook his head. "We couldn't go up there even if we did have time. Mr. Barstow would throw me out on my ear."

Red laughed. "How far is it from here?"

"Not far — just about two or three miles."

"On this same road?"

"Yes, on the other side of that high hill. If we drove to the top we could see it."

"Well, that hill is too steep for poor Bessie. If I ever want to see the Barstow ranch I guess I'll have to learn to ride a horse."

"I guess you will. Maybe I can give you a lesson after supper."

"That'd be fine," Red said. "I'd like that."

They climbed into Bessie and arrived back at the BW just in time to wash up for the evening meal. When Pete yelled "Come an' git it!" nobody held back. There were four healthy appetites at the table, and Pete's good food disappeared in record time.

While they were all drinking their coffee on the porch, Jim picked up the newspaper and pointed to an advertisement on the back page. "This should interest you, Red. There's a new western movie showing in town tomorrow night."

Red looked at the ad. "Hm, sounds good. Look at this picture, Joey — plenty of gunplay."

Joey looked at the photo of a tall, grim sheriff facing a dozen evil-looking men with smoking forty-fives in their hands. "Boy, I'd sure like to see this movie." He turned to Jim. "Let's all go tomorrow night."

"I'd like to, Joey," Jim said, "but tomorrow's the night when Pete and I have to go over our books to see if they balance. But you and Red could go. How about it, Red? You think poor Bessie could survive a trip to town?"

"I guess she could, Jim, if it's downhill both ways. What do you say, Joey, is it a date?"

"Sure."

Red studied the picture in the ad and shook his head. "I wonder if I'll ever be able to handle a gun like these fellows."

"You'd better learn," Jim said, "if you ever hope

to become a star in westerns. Have you ever fired a gun?"

"No, but I think I could get the hang of it pretty quickly."

Pete gave a grunt. "Pistol-shootin' ain't anywhere near as easy as these here movie fellers make it look. If you ask me, you better first learn how to fire a rifle."

"I've got a rifle, Red," Joey said eagerly, "a twenty-two. Jim and Pete gave it to me for Christmas. Before the riding lesson, what if I show you how to handle a rifle?"

"Whatever you say, teacher," Red agreed.

Joey raced into the house and brought out his rifle and a box of cartridges. "Okay, Red, let's go," he said breathlessly. "We'll practice shooting tin cans off that stump in back of the barn."

"Calm down, Joey," Jim warned. "When you're handling a weapon you've got to have all your wits about you."

"I'll be careful," Joey promised. He took Red to the barn, where they picked up a carton of empty cans and carried them out back to the stump. "Do you have any idea how a rifle works?" Joey asked.

"You'd better show me," Red suggested. "First let me see you shoot, then explain it to me."

"Okay, it isn't really hard once you get the hang of it."

Joey set a tin can on the stump, then came back and loaded his rifle. Aiming from a standing position, he shot the can squarely in the middle and sent it flying.

"Say, you're good, you know that?" Red said appreciatively.

Joey was pleased by Red's praise. "Well, I've had a lot of practice. Now before you try it, let me set up some more targets and show you how to shoot from other positions." Squatting at first, then lying prone, he drilled neat holes in two more cans.

Red applauded. "Annie Oakley had nothing on you, boy."

Joey laughed and placed another can on the stump. "Okay, now it's your turn." He inserted a cartridge and handed the rifle to Red.

Red took it gingerly. "What do I do?"

"You just line up these two sights on the can and shoot. But don't *pull* the trigger, because that jerks the gun and ruins your aim. Just squeeze it, and your aim will be steadier."

Red raised the rifle to his shoulder and took aim.

"Hey, wait a minute," Joey said, trying not to laugh. "You closed the wrong eye."

"I did?"

"Yes, you've got to shut the left one, not the right one."

"Oh," said Red, "no wonder I couldn't line that can up in the sights."

Under Joey's patient guidance, Red tried five or six shots from different positions, but never once came even close to hitting the target.

"Gosh darn it," he said disgustedly, "I guess I'm just not cut out to be a gunslinger." He handed the rifle back to Joey. "Here, teacher, mark me zero in rifle-shooting and give me a lesson in riding."

"Okay," Joey said, "but don't be discouraged. When I first fired a rifle I was as bad as you — almost." He grinned and took Red into the barn. "Now, before you try riding you'd better learn how to put a saddle on." He studied several horses standing patiently in their stalls. "Let's see — I want to pick you a nice gentle one."

"They all *look* gentle," Red said, "but I imagine the looks of horses can be somewhat deceiving. I don't want to get tossed, like that bronc-peeler we saw this afternoon at the Lazy M."

"We'll try Cactus," Joey decided, "he's Pete's horse. Cactus never threw anybody." He slipped a bridle on the quiet gelding and led him from the stall. "Now I'll show you how to saddle him."

The obedient Cactus stood still as Joey threw the saddle on his back and tightened the cinches. Red Baker watched the procedure with apparent interest.

"Okay," Joey said when all was ready, "now you can mount him. Just grab the saddle horn, put your foot in the stirrup and swing yourself up."

Red took a deep breath as if to gather courage, and approached Cactus warily. As he reached for the saddle horn, Joey stopped him with a shout.

"Wait! That's the wrong side!"

Red drew his hand back. "What do you mean?"

"That's the *right* side."

Red frowned. "But you just said it's the wrong side."

Joey laughed. "I know, but when you're mounting a horse, the right side *is* the wrong side. The *left* side is the right side."

"Huh? Oh — now I see what you mean." Red grinned at his own stupidity and came around to Cactus's left. After losing the stirrup on the first attempt, he finally managed to get a good foothold and swung unsteadily into the saddle.

"That's it," Joey said happily. "Now you look like a real cowboy."

"I don't feel like one. What do I do now?"

"Just sit still. I'll walk Cactus around a little until you get used to your seat."

Joey took hold of the bridle and led the gelding from the barn. Red buried his fingers in the brown mane and held on grimly.

"Jim — Pete — look!" Joey cried, as he walked Cactus toward the porch.

"Nice going, Red," Jim called. "You're really riding, cowboy!"

Pete watched the performance with disdain. "Ridin'?" he muttered. "I call it sittin'. A newborn baby could do what that fake cowboy's doin'."

"Quiet, Pete," Jim warned in a low voice. "He'll hear you."

"So what if he does?" Pete grumbled. "Right now I wisht that was a real cactus he's sittin' on."

Joey led the horse past the porch and down the road to Fury's corral, then eased him around and returned him to the barn. "Okay, Red, get down. I guess that's enough for the first lesson. Maybe tomorrow you can really ride."

"I hope so." Red slid to the ground. "Thanks, Cactus, you were very patient with me. You were, too, Joey."

Joey unsaddled the gelding and backed him into his stall. "Well, Red," he said, dropping the wooden catch bar, "it'll be dark in a little while. What shall we do till then?"

"Well, let me see — I think the time has come to reward the teacher. How would you like to hear 'The Ballad of Fury'?"

Joey's eyes popped open with pleasure. "You mean you've got it all finished?"

Red nodded. "I worked on it last night in the bunkhouse, after you went to bed."

Joey grabbed him by the arm. "Boy, that's wonderful! Come on, let's get your guitar."

They got the instrument from the bunkhouse and walked back toward the porch.

"Jumpin' Jee — hoshaphat!" Pete groaned when he saw the guitar in Red's hand. "Don't tell me we're gonna hafta lissen to more of that feller's caterwaulin'."

"Red's finished the song!" Joey cried gleefully. "Remember I told you he was going to write one about Fury? He's done it! It's called 'The Ballad of Fury'!"

"That's fine," Jim said. "Pete and I are anxious to hear it, aren't we, Pete?"

"Huh? Oh, yeah. Person'ly, my fav'rite tune's 'Home on the Range,' but I guess I won't mind lissenin' to this here one, seein' it's about Fury."

Red took a seat on the railing and tuned his guitar. "This is a story-song about how you captured Fury. Right after each verse, there's a chorus that we can all sing together. I'll sing it alone the first few

136

times when I get to it, then when you get the hang of it you can join in." He ran his fingers over the strings. "Okay, here goes: 'The Ballad of Fury.'" Red began singing in a pleasant baritone voice, and by the time he reached the third chorus, the others joined in lustily. The song went like this:

Early one spring to the hills I did ride
To find the wild horses that grazed the Divide,
I'd heard of their leader, a stallion so fine,
And black as the coal in an anthracite mine.

FU — RY! . . . . FU — RY!
From Oregon east to Miss — ou — ri,
Many fine horses are roaming the land,
But the king of them all is *Fury!*

I found the wild horses and sat there amazed,
For there stood the stallion on guard as they
    grazed,
An ebony giant — the king of his breed,
My heart ached to own this magnificent steed.

FU — RY! . . . . FU — RY!
From Oregon east to Miss — ou — ri,
Many fine horses are roaming the land,
But the king of them all is *Fury!*

The roan I was riding then pawed at the ground,
And all the wild horses looked up at the sound,
The stallion gave warning, and off raced the
    herd,
With thundering hoofs and the speed of a bird.

FU — RY! . . . . FU — RY!
From Oregon east to Miss — ou — ri,
Many fine horses are roaming the land,
But the king of them all is *Fury!*

The giant black stallion breathed fire at me,
But I could not rope him, so clever was he,
So I said, "All right, my magnificent pal,
One day you'll be standing inside my corral."

FU — RY! . . . . FU — RY!
From Oregon east to Miss — ou — ri,
Many fine horses are roaming the land,
But the king of them all is *Fury!*

I caught two mare mustangs and used them as
    bait,
Corraled them at midnight and sat down to wait,
And when I heard hoofbeats that tingled my
    spine,
The stallion came searching, and Fury was
    mine!

FU — RY! . . . . FU — RY!
From Oregon east to Miss — ou — ri,
Many fine horses are roaming the land,
But the king of them all is *Fury!*

Now many good ranchers come riding this way
To look at my stallion, and all of them say:
"I've seen many horses, and owned quite a few,
But Fury's the finest the world ever knew!"

FU — RY! . . . . FU — RY!
From Oregon east to Miss — ou — ri,
Many fine horses are roaming the land,
But the king of them all is *Fury!*

As the song ended, with a flashy strumming of the strings, everyone applauded. Even Pete, who had listened with increasing interest and had joined the last chorus, beat his calloused palms together. Red stood up and took a bow.

"That's wonderful!" Joey cried ecstatically. "Just wonderful!"

"It was great," Jim said. "Congratulations, Red."

Red was pleased. "Thanks — thanks very much." He glanced sideways at Pete, as if to hear his opinion.

"Yep, it's a good song," Pete admitted. " 'Twasn't no 'Home on the Range,' but it was okay."

Joey ran down the porch steps. "Come on, everybody — let's go sing it to Fury."

Good-naturedly, the men followed Joey to the corral. The hero of the song cantered to the fence to welcome the serenaders, and listened politely as they sang his ballad from beginning to end. After it was over, Joey insisted that during the final chorus he had seen Fury swing his head from side to side in time with the music.

"Aw, go on," Pete scoffed. "Fury's smart, but he ain't *that* smart."

Jim and Red remained silent. Both of them believed, without daring to admit it, that they too had seen Fury's head swaying to the rhythm. Pete believed it also but, like the others, he explained it to himself as an optical illusion caused by the lengthening shadows of dusk.

Chapter 11

THE MYSTERY OF RED BAKER

The following evening, as soon as supper was over, Jim took Red Baker aside to discuss the important subject of money. "If you and Joey are going to town to see that western movie tonight, I suppose you'll need an advance on your pay."

Red patted his empty pockets. "I sure will, Jim. I was going to ask you for it, but you beat me to it. I hate to stick you for money before payday, but as Pete would say, I'm 'plumb busted.' "

Jim took several bills from his wallet. "Be sure to let Joey pay his own way into the movie. He gets a salary for helping us work the ranch."

"Okay, we'll go Dutch." Red examined the paper money and grinned mischievously. "You sure these aren't some of the bills stolen from that bank robbery? I'd hate to be arrested and accused of being the thief."

Jim laughed. "You'll be perfectly safe. I printed that money this morning on my own private press." He grew serious. "If that bank robber is still in the valley, I don't think he'd be foolish enough to spend any more of his hot money. The ten-dollar bill that turned up at Matt Castle's got him too much publicity."

"It sure did. Are the police working on the case?"

"I imagine they are, but if the man's still around he'll be tough to find. This valley makes a perfect hiding place for a criminal. Hundreds of cowhands drift in and out, and it's impossible to check on every one of them."

"You're right. I don't see how it could be done." Red put the money in his pocket. "Thanks a lot, Jim, I appreciate your thoughtfulness."

"Don't mention it. Hope you enjoy the picture."

Red and Joey piled into Bessie and coasted down the hill with the motor off so as not to spook Fury. As they went by the corral, Fury threw his ears forward in apparent amazement at not hearing the jalopy's usual loud noise.

"Hey, Fury, don't look so surprised," Red called out. "Bessie can be a silent, charming lady when she feels like it." He started the motor after they coasted through the gate, and the old car transported them to town with a minimum of coughing and sputtering.

At the crowded movie theater they managed to find seats in the sixth row of the balcony and settled back to enjoy the picture. Soon after it began, a latecomer shuffled noisily into the row behind them. The man brushed both Joey and Red on the backs of their heads as he was finding his seat. Neither of them looked around, but they heard the man sit down directly behind Joey. The picture was a lively one, and Joey and Red soon found themselves engrossed. After it had been running for about ten minutes, Joey was jolted back to reality when the man behind him placed a heavy, booted foot on the back of his chair, right close to his ear. Without turning, Joey raised his hand and gave the foot a polite tap. His reminder that he was being annoyed went unheeded. The offender merely gave a grunt and kept his foot where it was. A moment later his other foot came up on the opposite side of Joey's seat. The man squirmed and twisted, and each time he moved, Joey was jostled violently.

When he could stand it no longer, he half turned in his seat and whispered, "Mister, will you *please* take your feet down?"

"Shut up, kid," came the hoarse answer.

There was something about the man's nasty tone that sounded familiar to Joey. He turned and looked up. In the dim light reflected from the screen he saw that the man who had been annoying him was Chick Lacy.

"Turn around, kid," Chick drawled. "Mind yer own business."

"But your feet are right against my head."

Chick leaned forward. "So what?" he said roughly. "Jest turn around and shut up!" Suddenly he recognized Joey, and his small eyes gleamed with malice. "Wal, wal," he rasped huskily, "if it ain't Jim Newton's brat."

The people in the vicinity were making shushing sounds. Red Baker, who had been aware of his companion's discomfort, pushed Chick's feet from the back of Joey's chair.

"Look," he said firmly, "you're annoying my friend and lots of others, so kindly keep your feet where they belong."

Lacy squinted down at Red. "Who're you, Mack, this dopey kid's keeper?"

"Never mind. Just keep your feet down and be quiet."

Lacy gave the back of Red's seat a kick with his heavy boot. His aim was faulty, and as the foot slipped forward over the top of the seat and brushed Red's ear, Red caught it and gave it a violent twist. Lacy roared with pain and outrage. As the audience demanded silence, Red took Joey by the arm.

"Come on, let's find other seats."

Chick shook his fist at them as they edged into the aisle. An usher had come down to investigate the disturbance.

"A man was annoying us," Red explained in a low voice. "Are there two other seats somewhere?"

The usher pointed with his flashlight. "Up there in the back row."

"Who was that tough character?" Red whispered to Joey, as they climbed the steps.

"Chick Lacy."

Red looked back over his shoulder. "Hm — he acts real nasty."

They slipped into their new seats and watched the remainder of the film without further incident. When the lights came on, and the audience was filing out, Red Baker peered down through the crowd and located Lacy. The jeep driver was craning his neck, apparently looking for Red and Joey, but couldn't spot them in the moving throng.

"I'd like to get a closer look at our nasty friend," Red told Joey. "Maybe we'll see him outside."

"I hope we don't. He's as mean as they come."

When they emerged from the theater Chick was nowhere to be seen, and Red seemed disappointed. "Let's go over to that drugstore and have a soda before we drive home," he suggested. "I doubt that Chick Lacy drinks sodas, but he just might be in there."

Joey frowned. "Why're you so anxious to see that guy? He's a real drag."

"He's part of my western education," Red grinned. "If I'm going to be a western hero, I've got to see what a western villain looks like up close."

After they had drunk their sodas without seeing Chick, they walked back to the lot where they had left Bessie. The jalopy was parked under one of the brilliant spotlights. Joey got in on his side and Red walked around to the driver's side. Just as he reached out to grasp the door handle a tall figure appeared from behind another car.

"Red!" Joey cried. "Look out — it's Chick Lacy!"

Red whirled. "What're you doing here, Lacy?"

The jeep driver hooked his thumbs in his greasy leather belt. "I got somethin' to settle with you, Mack. You come close to bustin' my ankle back there in the movie."

"You had it coming to you," Red said coldly. "You were annoying my young friend here."

Chick fixed his sleepy eyes on Joey. "You need a good beatin' yerself, kid — you an' Jim Newton both — fer gittin' the sheriff on my neck."

"But we didn't," Joey said. "Jim told you we didn't."

Red Baker was studying the jeep driver's sneering face. "Look, Lacy, I don't like threatening talk, so go away and leave us alone."

Red turned his back and reached for the door handle of the car. Before the fingers made contact, Chick leaped forward and swung his right fist. The powerful blow caught Red just behind his ear, and he went sprawling onto the cinders of the parking lot. Joey watched in horror as Chick lunged toward the fallen man. With a writhing motion, Red eluded his assailant and sprang to his feet. As he came up, still facing away from Chick, his attacker seized him by the hair and pulled back. With a lightning gesture, Red grabbed Lacy's right wrist with both hands, forcing him to keep the hold on his hair. Turning inward suddenly, pivoting on the ball of his left foot, he twisted Lacy's arm and stepped backward with his own right foot. In a continuous motion, he jerked his opponent's hand from his head in a downward and backward direction. Caught off balance, and unable to bear the pain of the arm twist, Lacy was catapulted forward on his face.

"Boy!" Joey shouted. "That was neat!"

Red was waiting calmly for Chick's next move. Chick staggered to his feet, rushed forward, and caught him in a bear hug. It was exactly what Red had been waiting for. Placing his left hand in the small of Lacy's back, he applied a vicious chin jab with the heel of his open right hand. As Chick received the crushing blow, his arms fell free. He was half out on his feet, but he plunged forward again, gasping for air. As he raised his fists, Red sidestepped and delivered a sharp, edge-of-the-hand blow on the biceps of his right arm. Lacy yelped with pain and sank to his knees, grasping his right arm with the other hand.

Red leaned down and tilted the groaning man's head back. In the overhead light, he studied the contorted face for a full ten seconds. "Have you had enough?" he asked finally. Lacy nodded vigorously. "Okay, Joey," Red said, wiping his hands on his jeans, "let's see if Bessie can make it home."

The clean defeat of Chick Lacy increased Joey's already vast admiration for Red Baker. In the morning, he was so excited when describing the battle to Jim and Pete, he could hardly finish his breakfast.

Jim was impressed by the ease with which Red had accomplished his victory. "That Lacy looks like a tough brawler. How're your fists this morning?"

"He didn't use his fists once," Joey exclaimed breathlessly. "And he never got hit, either, except at first when Chick slugged him when his back was turned."

Pete was puzzled. "I don't savvy this, Red. If you din use yer dukes, then how'd you win?"

Red smiled. "Well, when he caught me by the hair

I gave him an arm twist. Then I broke his bear hug with a chin jab, and finished him off with an edge-of-the-hand chop."

Pete winced. "When he grabbed you by the hair, din you lose none?"

Red rubbed his head. "Yes, I think I did, but I didn't notice it at the time."

Jim smiled reminiscently. "So you beat him with judo, eh? I learned a few tricks myself during Air Force training. Where did you learn judo, Red?"

Red hesitated for a fraction of a second. "Oh, I once bought a mail-order course and practiced on my little brother." He turned to Joey. "You ought to learn some of those tricks, Joey. A fellow with a little knowledge of judo can beat an unskilled brawler any time."

"I'd like to learn some," Joey said eagerly. "Will you teach me?"

"Sure — if I'm here long enough."

Jim got up from the table. "Well, slaves, let's go and fill the water troughs; I'd like to get the job done by noon. There's no letup in the dry spell, so Pete and I are going to ride up to the hills right after lunch and check the herd."

"May I go with you?" Joey asked.

"Sure, you'll be a big help to us."

The troughs were filled shortly before twelve, and after a quick lunch and a few chores, Jim and Pete went out and saddled their horses.

"Where's Joey?" Jim asked Red, who had followed them to the barn.

"I don't know, Jim, I haven't seen him for five or ten minutes."

Jim called Joey's name, and when he received no answer he was slightly annoyed. "When I mentioned this ride a little while ago he was eager to go along."

"Wal, that's the way boys are," Pete said. "You never know what they're gonna do from one minute to the next. Mebbe he plumb fergot about it an' rode over to see one of his school friends."

Red looked out of the barn. "He couldn't have gone riding — Fury's still in his corral."

"Hey," Pete said suddenly, "I bet I know where he went — out to find the bobcat that's been stealin' our chickens. Now that I think of it, I seen him through the door of his room when I come outa the kitchen. He was foolin' with his rifle."

"Well," Jim decided, "we'll have to go without him." He mounted his horse. "Let's get started, Pete, we've got a long ride ahead of us."

"How long will you be gone?" Red asked.

"Till sundown at least. We'll leave the ranch in your care."

Red smiled. "Okay, Jim, I'll try not to break anything." He walked from the barn, then turned. "Do you think there's any chance that Joey will be back soon?"

"I doubt it, Red. When he goes out to trail a bobcat he's usually gone for hours."

"That's right," Pete agreed, swinging into his saddle. "Joey never gives up on them critters. Sometimes he follows 'em fer miles an' don't git back till after dark."

"I hate to leave without him," Jim said, "but I've got to — I'm worried about the herd. What with the drought, and Barstow's airplane scaring them out of their wits, there's no telling what kind of condition they're in." He slapped his rein. "Let's go, Pete."

"I'm right on yer tail, boss."

They said so-long to Red and rode off. Red watched them until they were far out on the range. When they had disappeared around an outcropping of rock, he moved quickly and purposefully to the house and called Joey's name. There was no answer, either from the house or any of the outbuildings. Satisfied that he had the ranch to himself, Red hurried to the bunkhouse and opened one of his suitcases. From beneath a pile of shirts he took out an automatic pistol and a dozen clips of shells. Going swiftly to the barn, he packed a carton with empty tin cans and carried it back to the stump where he and Joey had practiced with the rifle.

A few minutes later, Fury heard the repeated crack of the pistol and jerked his head up in alarm. Having lived with humans for only a short span of his life, the stallion had never become fully accustomed to the sound of shooting, which in his experience was always associated with trouble. A shudder ran through his great body as the firing continued, and instinctively he knew that he should seek the protection of the boy who had won his confidence and given him loving care. With his mane and tail flying wildly in the wind, he raced around his enclosure, seeking a way out. Finding none, he swung toward the center of the corral, gathered speed, and leaped the opposite fence. He had seen the boy leave the house and cut across the meadow, so he knew exactly in which direction he should go to find him.

Pete's hunch about Joey's disappearance had been correct. Joey had taken his rifle and gone off to trail the bobcat. He was fairly certain that the cat was not too far away, and would be found in a clump of cedars on the wagon road just south of the ranch. Several hundred yards from the edge of the meadow he found the remains of the chicken which the animal had stolen that morning. The tracks of the cat's broad pads, and an occasional chicken feather, led straight to the cedars. In the excitement of the hunt, Joey forgot the ride which Jim had planned, and stalked the bobcat for quite some time without finding it. Disappointed at losing his quarry, he sat down on a flat rock and wondered where he himself would be hiding if he were the bobcat. Finally, when a shaft of sunlight pierced the treetops and reflected from the barrel of his rifle, he suddenly remembered the ride, and realized that he would miss it unless he hurried back to the ranch. With a last look upward, in the hope of seeing the bobcat crouched in the overhead branches, he abandoned the hunt and started back. As he reached the wagon road he heard hoofbeats, and hoped that the rider would be Jim, coming to fetch him. To his amazement, the riderless horse that came galloping around the bend was Fury. Joey stood in the middle of the road and waved his arms, and as Fury came to a stop and pranced about, he knew from experience that the stallion's agitation had been caused by something out of the ordinary. Fury rolled his eyes upward, and punctuated his wild dance with a series of startling snorts.

Joey grasped his mane in an attempt to settle him down. "What is it, Fury — what happened?"

Fury jerked his head up, breaking Joey's hold, and turned back toward the ranch. After running ten or fifteen yards, he whirled and whinnied pleadingly.

Joey ran to him and caught his mane again. "Did you jump your corral? Has something happened?" As if in answer, Fury made a strange, impatient sound. "Okay, then — let's go back!"

Taking a firmer grasp on the mane, Joey pulled himself up to Fury's bare back and swung his right leg over. "Come on!" he cried, bringing his knees in against the ribs. "Let's hurry!"

They were moving at top speed as they approached the ranch gate, and as they passed through, Joey heard the sound of pistol shots, coming from behind the barn.

"Hey," he murmured in Fury's ear, "I wonder if that's Jim."

It occurred to him that perhaps Jim had canceled the ride to the uplands and was giving Red Baker a shooting lesson. He jumped down and led Fury into his corral. After closing the gate, he ran up the road, eager to find out how Red was doing. As he reached the grass that bordered the barn, another series of shots rang out in rapid succession, and he saw tin cans flying through the air. To his great surprise, Red Baker came into view, moving away from Joey toward the stump to set the targets up again. Red had an automatic pistol in his hand, and Joey realized to his stunned amazement that it was Red who had done the magnificent shooting. He wanted to call out to Red, but owing to his astonishment he was unable to use his voice.

Because Red stood with his back to Joey while setting up the targets, he was unaware that he was being watched. Joey's legs felt suddenly weak, and he sank to the ground behind the piled-up water drums. When he heard Red returning to the firing line, he crouched lower and peeked out between two of the drums. He saw Red examine his pistol with satisfaction and insert another clip into the chamber. Turning quickly, Red fired from the hip, and again blasted the row of cans from the stump.

At this second demonstration of Red's skill, Joey felt completely wretched. The young stranger whom he had liked and trusted had deceived him. Red had claimed that he had never handled a firearm in his life, yet the perfect performance which Joey had just witnessed proved that claim to be an outright lie. Sick at heart, he peered through the crack again and watched Red's actions. Red gathered the perforated cans and the ejected shells, stuffed them into the carton, and buried the carton under the trash pile. That chore completed, he glanced about the ranch, as if to make sure he was not being watched, then hurried back to the barn. Joey was determined now not to be seen, and as he squatted behind the drums, Red loped past his hiding place and entered the barn. As Joey pressed his ear against the wooden wall, he recognized the sound of a saddle being lifted from the rack, then the hollow thud of a horse's hoofs as he was being led from the stall.

Red's muffled voice reached his ear. "Hold it, boy — stand still. That's right — we'll get you saddled in two seconds."

A moment later, Joey heard the horse move from the barn, then saw it canter down the hill with Red seated easily in the saddle. Red waved gaily to Fury as he passed the corral, and when he reached the dirt road he headed north up the valley.

Joey rose unsteadily to his feet and watched the rider until he had turned the first bend. He shook his head in complete bewilderment. Red Baker could ride as well as he could shoot. But why had he lied to everybody — why? Too miserable to find the answer, Joey walked dejectedly down the road to the corral, where he knew he would find a true friend.

Chapter 12
JOEY LEAVES THE BW

When Red Baker arrived at the hilltop beyond the Lazy M and the Triple X, he brought his horse to a halt and studied the terrain ahead. Spread out from the bottom of the hill to the base of the ridge beyond lay a vast ranch. On the water tower he saw the name, BARSTOW, printed in large, black letters. He slapped his rein and continued down the hill to the gate. A short distance up the driveway, a small boy, dressed in expensive chaps and a ten-gallon hat, was throwing a lasso at a fencepost. The boy turned around as Red rode up and greeted him.

"Hi, fella — you're pretty good with that loop."

The boy looked up with a friendly smile. "Thanks. My dad makes me practice every day."

"Good idea. My name's Red Baker, what's yours?"

"David Barstow."

Red glanced at the water tower. "The boss's son?"

"Yes, sir. If you came to see my dad, he's way up in the north pasture."

"Thanks, but I'm looking for Chick Lacy."

David frowned. "Oh — he's up in the bunkhouse. He's not feeling so good today."

Red suppressed a grin. "I'm sorry to hear that. Where is the bunkhouse?"

David pointed. "Up there on the other side of the stables."

"Thanks a lot, David. Good luck with your roping." Red clucked and rode up the hill. After dismounting and tying his leather to the hitch-rail, he entered the open door of the bunkhouse. It was empty, except for one man who lay sleeping at the far end of the room. Even in the dim light, Red recognized the sprawling man as Chick Lacy. As he walked toward the bunk, Lacy opened one sleepy eye. Red greeted him with a grin. "Hi, Lacy."

The jeep driver recognized him and sprang to a sitting position. As he did so, he uttered a cry of pain and clutched his back.

"Sorry about your back," Red said. "It must hurt a lot."

There was a look of hatred in Lacy's eyes. "Leave me alone!" he shouted. "Git outa here an' leave me alone!" He glanced quickly at his rifle, which stood against the wall just beyond his reach.

"No need to go for the iron," Red said with a chuckle. "This is a friendly visit." He picked up the rifle and tossed it onto another bunk.

Chick rose stiffly to his feet and backed up to the

wall. "Whattaya want?" he muttered. "Ya done enough to me last night. Git out an' leave me alone!"

"I'm not going to touch you, Lacy. I'm glad to see you on your feet with no broken bones."

Chick squinted at Red suspiciously. "Whattaya mean yer glad? Ya like to busted my back last night."

"What did you expect me to do after you socked me in the head?"

Chick looked away. "Awright, awright — so ya paid me off. So whattaya want now?"

"I was riding by, and I thought I'd drop in to see how you were feeling."

Lacy rubbed his right arm. "I feel lousy, that's how I'm feelin'."

"Well, at least you're up and around," Red said. "By tomorrow you'll be as good as new."

The jeep driver shook his head. "Look, Mack, I don't git this. Last night ya beat me up — today ya wanta know how I'm feelin'. What's the idea?"

Red motioned to the bunk. "Sit down, friend — it must hurt to stand." Lacy lowered himself with a groan. "I mussed you up pretty badly last night," Red continued, "and I want to tell you I'm sorry I had to be so rough."

Chick ran his fingers through his untidy black hair and reached painfully for a pack of cigarettes.

"Here," Red said quickly, "have one of mine." He took a pack from his shirt pocket and tossed it to Chick, who caught it and extracted a cigarette with a shaking hand. Red leaned down and retrieved the pack and returned it carefully to his pocket. He scratched a match and held it out. "Here, have a light." Lacy took a deep draw and blew out a cloud of smoke. Red extended his hand. "No hard feelings?".

Lacy glared at the outstretched hand and curled his lip. "Git lost," he growled sullenly.

"Okay," Red said calmly, "I'll see you around." He turned and walked quickly from the bunkhouse. As he cantered down the road he gave David a friendly wave. "So long, David. Keep practicing with that rope."

"I will, Mr. Baker," David called. "So long."

The boy watched the rider as he passed through the gate. As the horse turned left, David saw the man wrap some small object in a white handkerchief. When the horse broke into a gallop, the lonely boy sighed and went back to his roping.

An hour later, Red Baker swung into the Broken Wheel, unseen by anyone but Joey, who had been watching for his return from a window of the ranch house. In the barn, Red unsaddled the sweating horse, gave him a quick rubdown with a sponge, and backed him into the stall. Moving with swift strides, he proceeded from the barn to the bunkhouse and closed the door. For the next half hour he was busily occupied with the object in the white handkerchief.

Jim and Pete returned shortly after sunset. Joey greeted them glumly and returned to his room.

"What in tarnation's eatin' *him?*" Pete said. "His face looks like a spoiled tomater."

"I guess he's a little miffed about our going off without him," Jim surmised. "He'll get over it."

At supper, Joey took his place at the table but

hardly touched his food. When anyone addressed him, he answered in monosyllables. Jim asked him if it was true that he had gone bobcat-hunting, and he said yes. When Pete wanted to know if he had shot the bobcat, he answered no. The three men at the table exchanged glances and decided silently that Joey was in a mood and would probably come out of it if they left him alone.

For the rest of the meal, Red Baker did most of the talking. Hoping to interest Joey, he told lively anecdotes about the nightclubs in which he had played and sung, but Joey remained tight-lipped and refused even to look at Red while he was speaking.

After supper, Jim whispered to Red to get his guitar. "Maybe Joey will snap out of it," he said, "if you sing 'The Ballad of Fury' again."

"I hope so," Red said, "he's certainly bugged about something."

"He looks as sour as an undertaker's assistant," Pete said in a low voice. "Go on, Red — fetch that ole *git*-tar an' we'll raise the roof."

During the songfest, Joey sat on the top step of the porch with his back to the group. When Red sang the "Ballad," he joined in the chorus, but without much enthusiasm. As soon as the song was over, he excused himself and went to his room.

Pete slapped the arm of his rocker. "Goldern it, that ain't like Joey. Somethin's spooked him fer shore."

Jim was concerned. "You're right." He turned to Red. "Did anything happen this afternoon while Pete and I were gone — anything that might've upset him?"

"Not that I know of, Jim. I must have been in the bunkhouse when he came back from the bobcat hunt. Matter of fact, I didn't see him at all till suppertime."

Jim stood up. "Well, something's bothering him, and I can't let him go to bed without getting it off his chest. I'm going in and have a talk with him."

He found Joey at his bedroom window, staring out at Fury's corral. Jim laid his arm gently on the boy's shoulder. "All right, son, let's talk things out."

"I don't know what you mean," Joey said, without turning.

Jim drew up a chair and sat down. "Sure you do." He took Joey's hand. "After you became my son last year we agreed that we'd never keep secrets from each other, isn't that so?" Joey nodded. "All right, then, let's keep to our bargain." He drew the boy toward him and looked him full in the face. "Are you angry because we rode off without you this afternoon?" Joey didn't answer. "We couldn't wait for you, you know that. Our main job is to look after our horses."

"That wasn't it," Joey murmured, "that wasn't it at all." There were tears in his eyes.

"Very well, son — tell me the real reason."

Joey took a deep, sobbing breath and fell to his knees beside the chair. "It was Red," he gasped. "He's a liar and a cheat!" As Jim listened in shocked surprise, the boy poured out the incredible story of Red's mysterious actions. "Why did he fool us that way?" Joey sobbed when he had finished. "Why did he lie to us, Jim? Why did he tell us he couldn't ride or shoot?"

Jim shook his head and rose to his feet. "I don't know, Joey — what you've told me shocks me very much." He paced back and forth across the room, then stopped and patted the miserable boy on the shoulder. "Look, son, I feel bad, too. I liked Red myself — almost as much as you did. I thought he was a fine man — a real gentleman. But now I hardly know what to think."

"I hate him!" Joey said vehemently. "He's a liar."

Jim made a decision. "You wait here. I'm going out and have a showdown."

Joey followed him to the door. "Afterwards, will you come back here and tell me what happened?"

"I sure will, Joey. You deserve an explanation before any of the rest of us."

As Jim returned to the porch, Pete looked up eagerly. "What was it, Jim? Did ya find out what was spookin' him?"

Jim nodded. "Yes, Pete, and it's pretty serious. You'll have to excuse Red and me — we're going down the road for a private talk."

Pete bristled. "A *private* talk? What's so dang private that *I* can't lissen?"

"I'll tell you later. Come on, Red."

Red followed Jim down the steps. "I think I know what this is about, Jim."

"I'm sure you do," Jim said brusquely, "but hold it till we get away from the house."

They walked in silence until they reached the gate, where Jim turned and angrily demanded an explanation of Red's actions. In the still night air the two men talked for a long time. At the end of the conversation, Red walked up to the bunkhouse, and Jim went to his room and closed the door. Pete had already gone to his own room, in a huff at not having been invited to join the discussion. Jim lay down on his bed and stared at the ceiling, his mind in a turmoil, as he tried to decide what he would say to Joey.

In a few moments, Joey knocked lightly on the door and came in at Jim's invitation.

"Jim," he began anxiously, "what happened? You promised you'd come back and tell me."

Jim sat up. "I know I did, Joey, but now it's impossible. Please go back to your room and try to forget it."

Joey was hurt by Jim's refusal. "But you promised."

Jim heaved a sigh. "Look, son, this whole thing is a matter for grown-ups. So please drop it and go to bed."

Jim's unaccustomed bluntness turned Joey's feeling of distress to one of anger. As he turned on Jim, his voice was accusing. "You never talked this way to me before — *ever!* I'm not just a little kid that plays around all day; I work the ranch, just like you and Pete! I haul water — and I clean the stalls — and I — and I — " he was too wrought up to continue.

"Joey, Joey," Jim said imploringly, "please try to understand. I know that you're not just a little kid, and we couldn't get our work done without you. But now we've reached a crisis, and you must get over it like an adult." He placed his hands on Joey's shoulders. "When Red Baker came to the Broken Wheel we both liked him right away, but we put too much trust in him, too quickly. He was a total stranger, a drifter, and he deceived us. This experience teaches both of us one of life's grim lessons: people you take a sudden shine to, sometimes turn out to be disappointments."

Joey was about to speak, but Jim stopped him with a gesture. "Red's leaving the BW — he'll be gone within twenty-four hours. Meanwhile, I want your solemn word of honor that you won't be a tale-bearer."

"What do you mean?" Joey asked.

"You're not to tell anybody — not even Pete — about what you saw Red doing this afternoon. Will you give me your word?"

Joey looked up, bewildered. "But, Jim, why shouldn't I tell Pete?"

"Never mind — give me your promise."

Joey hesitated. "All right," he said in a low, pained voice, "I promise." He turned quickly and ran back to his own room.

Early the next morning, Pete scurried into Jim's room in his long, white nightshirt. "Jim!" he cried excitedly. "Wake up!" He grabbed Jim's pajama coat and yanked it violently.

Jim sat up sleepily. "What's the matter?"

"That Red Baker — he's been off the ranch somewheres! The noise of that car of his woke me up. When I looked out the winder, I seen him come through the gate an' drive up to the bunkhouse. An' when he got outa the car I seen him carryin' a big pair of field glasses."

Jim stood up. "Are you sure?"

"Shore I'm shore — ya think I'm blind?" Pete pounded the bureau. "Now where in tarnation's that feller been, an' who was he spyin' on?"

Jim was getting into his clothes. "I don't know, Pete. I'll go out and ask him."

Pete stomped up and down the room. "Jim, I don't trust that feller — never did since the day he come here. But you an' Joey — ya both been treatin' him like he was a long-lost cousin. I tell ya there's somethin' awful funny about that critter — he's gotta go!"

"Take it easy, Pete. Simmer down."

The old man glared. "Simmer *down?* How kin I simmer down?" He shook his finger under Jim's nose. "Fer all we know, that Red Baker's a crook — mebbe even a murderer on the lam!"

"I doubt that," Jim said calmly, "but I'll go out and have a talk with him. You stay in the house."

Pete exploded with anger. "Whattaya mean, stay in the house? Ya think I'm a little kid?" He thrust his whiskered chin up into Jim's face. "An' while we're at it, Jim Newton, how come ya treated me the way ya done last night, when ya cut me outa that private talk? An' how come yer so high an' mighty right now — orderin' me to stay in the house?"

Jim sighed. "You don't understand, Pete. I only — "

"I don't understand, don't I? Wal, there's one thing I *do* understand — yer givin' me crackpot orders that don't make no sense! If I ain't wanted around this ranch, I'll be only too glad to pack up an' git out!"

Jim himself was getting riled by Pete's cranky jab-

164

ber. "Act your age!" he snapped. "You're behaving like a child! Red Baker will be gone by nightfall — maybe sooner."

"He ain't the only one that'll be gone!" Pete yelled. "I'll be gone meself — jest as soon as I kin git packed!" He stomped to the doorway and turned. "Ya kin find yerself a new foreman — one that don't behave like no child!"

After Pete had slammed the door of his own room, Jim threw some water on his face and went to the bunkhouse to see Red Baker. A few minutes later, Joey entered Pete's room fully dressed, and found the old man bunching up his clothes and heaving them into an old suitcase. He was still wearing his flapping nightshirt.

"Hey, Pete," Joey said in amazement, "what're you doing?"

"I'm packin', that's what I'm doin'! I'm leavin' this crazy layout ferever!"

"But why? What happened?"

Pete was rooting through his bureau drawers and throwing his belongings on the bed. "Everybody at the Broken Wheel has went plumb loco! First you, last night — broodin' an' sighin' like a sick calf — an' now Jim, talkin' to me like I was a kid in kindygarden! If ya ask me, yer a passel of lunatics — an' if I was to stay here another minute I'd be a lunatic meself!" He shook an old boot at Joey. "While we're on the subjeck — how come you was so fiddlefaced last night? What was eatin' ya?"

"I can't tell you," Joey said unhappily.

Pete fired the boot at the wall in exasperation. "Ya can't *tell* me? Whattaya mean ya can't tell me?"

"Jim made me promise not to mention it to anybody — not even you."

Pete blew his cheeks out like an angry monkey. "Wal now, ain't that jest dandy! Now even *yore* agin me!"

"I'm sorry, Pete, but I promised."

Pete threw his arms in the air. "What in the name of boiled catfish is goin' on around here? How come ya gotta keep stuff from *me?* What am I — human rat poison 'r somethin'?"

Joey toed the rug. "Gosh, Pete, I'm sorry you feel this way. I'd like to tell you, honest I would, but I just can't."

"Wal, that's great!" Pete said sarcastically. "Ya'd like to tell me, but ya jest can't. I'm jest the crazy uncle that's kept locked up in the attic 'cause he can't be trusted with fam'ly secrets. 'Pore, loony Uncle Pete,' they say behind me back. 'He was a fine feller before he got seeds in his pumpkin an' hadda be put in the squirrel factory.' " He balled up a suit of long, woolen underwear, stuffed it into a corner of his suitcase, closed the suitcase, and snapped the lock.

"Pete," Joey said dolefully, "are you really leaving the ranch?"

"What's it look like? I'm all packed, ain't I?" He jerked the heavy suitcase from the bed and started for the door. "Mebbe I'll send ya a postcard sometime — that is, if the keeper trusts me with a pencil."

"Wait a minute," Joey called. "You can't go like that."

"Why can't I?"

"You're still in your nightshirt."

Pete looked down at his white garment. "Dang it, so I am!" He stomped back to the bed and opened the suitcase. "Mebbe I *do* belong in a loony bin."

While Pete was pulling out a shirt and a pair of rumpled jeans, Joey heard a door slam. It was Jim, who had returned to his room. Joey ran out into the living room and came face to face with Red Baker. He attempted to pass Red without speaking, but Red caught him by the arm.

"Wait a second, Joey," he said gently, "I want to talk to you."

Joey glared up at his fallen hero. "What for?"

"Jim says you saw me shooting and riding yesterday."

"Yes!" Joey cried fiercely. "You're a fake, that's what you are! A fake and a phony!"

Red flushed. "No, Joey, don't say that — you don't understand. Maybe a little later you'll — "

"I won't see you a little later!" Joey broke in. "I'm going for a long ride, and maybe I'll never come back! Anyway, I hope I never see you again!"

He pulled his arm from Red's grasp and dashed from the house. Red stood on the porch and watched him with a troubled expression, as he saddled Fury and rode swiftly up the valley. With a sigh of regret, Red went to Jim's room and told him about Joey's leaving.

"He was pretty broken up, Jim. He said maybe he'd never come back."

Jim was alarmed. "I don't like this a bit." He hurried to Pete's bedroom. The irate old fellow was dressed and heading for the door with his suitcase.

"Where do you think you're going?" Jim demanded.

"I'm pullin' out fer good," Pete snapped. "Leave me by."

"Don't be a lunkhead!" Jim said angrily. "I've got enough trouble. Joey's gone."

Pete raised his eyebrows. "Gone where?"

"I don't know, but he said maybe he'd never come back. In his frame of mind, there's no telling what foolish thing he might do. If he isn't back by lunchtime, we'll have to go looking for him."

" 'We'? Who's 'we'?"

"You and I, Pete — Joey's good friends."

Pete set his suitcase down. "Okay, I'll stick with ya till he gits back. But then I'm leavin', like I said."

Jim compressed his lips. "Okay, Pete, if you want to go, I can't stop you."

He walked out to the porch and looked to the north, where the ridges were shimmering in a haze of heat and dust. The sun was blistering, and the land was parched. The brassy sky gave no promise of relief from the drought. Jim shuddered, then started down the road to see about the horses.

Chapter 13
FAIR WARNING

Fury's mane and tail streamed in the wind as his flashing hoofs pounded the hard-packed road. Joey had given him his head, and the joyful stallion took full advantage of his freedom to run without restraint. Since the drought had forced Joey to spend so much time hauling water, Fury had been denied his usual daily workout, and now he welcomed the opportunity to race at top speed.

Joey's only desire as he sped up the range was to get away from the valley — to ride northward as far as possible. He had no particular destination in mind. He knew only that he never wanted to see his false friends of the Broken Wheel again. Red Baker had deceived him. Pete had accused him unjustly of turning against him, and Jim — the man who had accepted him as a son — had broken his heart. It was Jim who had dealt the heaviest blow — there had been no reason for his harshness. Suddenly, and without cause, Jim had changed from a loving, understanding companion to a stern parent who treated Joey like a child. Only one true friend was left — his magnificent, half-wild stallion — and Joey knew that this friend would remain true always. He leaned forward in his saddle and caressed the black, muscular neck. "King of them all," he murmured. "King of them all is *Fury!*"

A mile above the Barstow ranch a narrow road bisected the main highway at right angles. As Joey approached it, he saw a red car equipped with a long radio antenna parked near the intersection. As he came closer, he recognized it as the firewarden's official vehicle. Bill Gibson, the warden, stepped into the road and held up his hand, and Joey reined in.

"What's up, Joey?" the warden asked anxiously. "Were you looking for me?"

"No, I wasn't looking for anybody." Joey hadn't wanted to be stopped and was slightly annoyed.

Bill glanced at Fury's sweating flanks. "The way you were highballing along, I thought maybe you'd discovered a fire somewhere."

Joey looked away in embarrassment. "No, Warden, there's no fire — at least, none that I know of."

The man frowned. "This is a mighty hot day to be riding so fast. Is there anything wrong at the BW?"

Joey hesitated before finding an answer. "Uh — not exactly. I — I just felt like getting away, that's all."

The warden smiled. "Oh, it's a private matter, eh?"

"Yes, sir, I don't feel like talking about it if you don't mind."

The man nodded understandingly. "Of course I don't mind." He reached up and grasped the boy's arm. "Is there anything I can do, Joey?"

"No, sir, thanks just the same." He sniffled and blew his nose. "Well, I guess I'll be going."

It was obvious to Bill Gibson that Joey was deeply troubled about something. He felt that the best way to snap Joey out of his despondent mood was to give him a job to do that would make him feel necessary and important. Bill grabbed Fury's bridle. "Wait a second, Joey. If you're not doing anything special, you can certainly give me a hand. How about it?" Joey looked doubtful. "I appointed you a Junior Forest Ranger," the warden went on, "because I have confidence in your judgment. Now I really need your help — if you have time."

Joey looked down at the man's friendly face. "Well, yes, sir, I do have time but — "

"Good. The whole range is dry as tinder. As you know, I closed the entire area to hunters and picnickers a few days ago. My men are patrolling the north end of the valley to stop them from coming in from that direction. Trouble is, I'm short handed, and you could give me valuable assistance today. So what do you say?"

Pleased by the warden's confidence, Joey smiled wanly. "Okay, if you really need me."

"I sure do." Bill pointed to the intersection. "This is one of the check points where we're turning the hunters back." He shook his head. "Doggone it,

Joey, if people would only realize the awful consequences of forest fire they'd be more careful. One tiny spark can destroy thousand of acres of valuable timberland. And the soil, too. Once the life-giving elements of the soil have been scorched, the land is ruined for years."

"I know," Joey said. "Fire kills the young growth and all the roots of the trees." He scowled. "It kills animals and people, too."

"Right. I hate to turn hunters back, but I have to, for their own good. Nobody can know how terrifying it is to be caught in the middle of a burning forest until he's actually had the experience. Then sometimes it's too late. Believe me, Joey, I've seen it, and I know what I'm talking about." The warden turned his head to the west, as a sudden movement caught his eye. An unexpected gust of hot wind was moving across the range, throwing up small funnels of dust and dead brush. "Uh-oh," he muttered, "this makes the danger even worse." He moved quickly to his car, flicked the radio switch and took the hand mike from its cradle. Joey slipped down from Fury's back and ran over to listen.

The warden twisted his body and watched the oncoming dust funnels as he spoke into the mike in a flat voice. "K-S-M to Lost Hill Tower . . . K-S-M to Lost Hill Tower . . . Come in, Thompson."

A voice came from the speaker on the dashboard. "Lost Hill Tower to K-S-M . . . Thompson here — go ahead, Bill."

"I'm at the check point on the north end road. We've got a sudden west wind. How's it look from up where you sit?"

172

"Hot, dry, and dangerous, but no smoke, thank goodness. I noticed the wind when it first kicked up. It's even stronger on the west side of the ridge. Gosh Bill, that's all we need in weather like this — wind."

"You said it. Have you seen any of my patrols though your binocs?"

"Yep, they're spreading out over Indian Mountain. Let's hope no dopes wander up there today with matches."

"Well, we're doing our best to keep them out. I've already turned back two carloads. They almost bit my head off — said I was spoiling their fun. . . . By the way, I've got a good man here to help me — Joey Newton, a Junior Ranger."

"That's great, Bill. Give him thumbs up for me."

"Hold it. I think Joey'd like to report in, too." The warden handed the mike to Joey.

Joey grinned uncertainly, then spoke into it. "Hi. Joey Newton, Junior Forest Ranger, reporting." He tried not to sound too excited. "My horse Fury and I are here helping Warden Gibson."

The voice from the tower rang out a welcome. "Glad to have you with us, ranger. I'll tell HQ you're on the job."

"Thank you, sir." Joey said, handing the mike back to Bill.

"Okay, Thompson," Bill said, "I'll keep in touch. K-S-M to tower — out." He replaced the mike and turned to Joey, who was smiling broadly.

"Boy," Joey said, "imagine talking all the way to Lost Hill Tower from here."

"Yes, this two-way radio's a big help in fire control work." The warden looked to the south and

shaded his eyes. A large, yellow convertible was bar-
reling toward the intersection, throwing up a cloud
of brown dust. He stepped into the center of the road
and raised his hand. As the car slowed down, Joey
recognized its two occupants.

"It's Mr. Barstow and David."

"Right," the warden muttered, "and there's two
rifles in the back seat. Brace yourself for a real, stiff
argument."

Barstow braked to a stop and leaned out. "What
is it, Warden?" he demanded brusquely.

Before Bill Gibson could answer, David stood up
in his seat and waved to Joey. "Hi, Joey!" he called
happily. "What're you doing out here?"

"I'm on fire duty — what're *you* doing?"

David glanced timidly at his father, who was glar-
ing at Joey.

"We're going hunting," Barstow announced. He
spoke sternly to the warden. "What did you stop us
for?"

Bill walked around to the driver's side. "Sorry,
Mr. Barstow, but this is a closed fire area. I'm afraid
you'll have to turn back."

Barstow was indignant. "Turn back? What kind of
nonsense is that?"

"The fire hazard is extreme," the warden explained politely. "We're requesting all hunters to
leave the area."

Barstow pounded the wheel. "But my son and I
have planned this hunt for days!"

Bill answered calmly. "I'm sure of that, sir, but so
have lots of others. Believe me, it's for your own
safety, as well as for the conservation of the land."

" 'For my own safety,' " Barstow mimicked. "Do you mean to tell us we don't know how to take care of ourselves?" He shook his finger under the warden's nose. "Young man, I was hunting when you were wearing knee pants, so don't try to class me with those tenderfeet that drive out from the city!"

The warden drew a deep breath. "Mr. Barstow, this valley is officially closed. I've requested you to call off your hunt — now it's an order."

Barstow was unaccustomed to taking orders, but there was a grim expression on the warden's face that caused him to back down slightly. "But I promised my son," he said in a less belligerent tone. He patted the boy's arm. "You don't want to turn back, do you, David?"

David was squirming with embarrassment. "Well, Dad," he said miserably, "I did want to go hunting, but on account of the fire danger I guess we'd better not. Joey told me how serious it was."

"*Joey* told you?" Barstow swung back to Joey, his anger mounting again. "Still meddling in my affairs, are you, boy?"

"No, Mr. Barstow," Joey began. "I only — "

"You and Jim Newton!" Barstow roared. "You're both alike! Because of your blasted mustangs you're bound and determined to cause me trouble."

"I'm sorry, Joey," David interrupted in a tortured voice. "I didn't mean to mention your name."

"That's okay," Joey said. "You were right to tell your dad what I said about not hunting during the drought. I was only carrying out the warden's request."

"Now, Mr. Barstow," the warden said sternly,

"we'd be obliged if you'd turn back and not give us any more trouble."

Barstow gave Joey a disgusted glance and threw his car into reverse. Backing into the intersecting road, he jerked the wheel around and turned the car in the opposite direction. He stepped hard on the accelerator, and the wheels spun up plumes of dust before they caught hold and propelled the car forward. As it roared past the warden's car, David gave Joey a feeble wave.

"So long," Joey called. "See you soon."

Warden Gibson took off his hat and scratched his head. "Joey," he said quizzically, "if Barstow ever mails me a mysterious package, remind me not to open it."

"What do you mean?"

"There's sure to be a bomb in it." He looked at Joey and grinned. "I'm not the only one he's sore at, either. I hear he also has it in for you and Jim."

Joey nodded. "He has it in for everybody — except David."

"I feel sorry for that boy. His dad keeps him wrapped up in cotton wool."

"Yes, he won't let him go anywhere or do anything. David's pretty lonely, I guess."

"I don't doubt it."

A carful of picnickers came up the road, and Bill Gibson had another argument before they gave in and turned back to town. He radio-checked the tower again and received an "all quiet" report. The wind had become steady and was blowing at eight to ten miles an hour. The valley was filled with a dust haze which coppered the air. Bill glanced at the sky.

"I don't like this wind, Joey. If a fire started anywhere, it could play us some nasty tricks."

"That's right — but the wind might break the heat, too."

"It's possible, but I don't see any rain clouds up there." Bill Gibson checked a few charts and changed the subject. "Seeing Barstow reminds me — how's Jim making out with his committee to save the mustangs?"

"Well, lately he hasn't had much time to work on it. Since our pumps went dry, we've been spending the mornings hauling water from the lake."

"Some job." Bill motioned to Fury, who was nibbling at a small clump of grass that had almost turned brown. "Do you suppose there's any more stallions like him up in the hills?"

"No, *sir*," Joey answered emphatically. "Not like Fury — he's something special. There's a lot of fine wild horses up there, though; but Mr. Barstow's killing them off."

"So I hear. That's Barstow's main gripe against Jim, isn't it — Jim's fight to save the mustangs?"

"Sure, but he blames Jim for something else, too."

"What's that?"

Joey told the warden about their visit to the Barstow ranch with the sheriff the morning after the arrest of the rustlers. He described Barstow's anger at Jim's having been invited to accompany the sheriff as a witness during the search of the bunkhouse. As Joey was relating the story, he realized suddenly that he was defending Jim, and when he remembered that he was running away from Jim forever, he stopped in confusion.

Another hunting party that had to be stopped and turned back saved him from further explanation. The warden watched the car driving down the road. "You know, Joey, whenever I see strangers I wonder about the man who spent the stolen ten-dollar bill at Matt Castle's store. I imagine the sheriff is still hunting for him, don't you?"

"Yes, I guess he is. He'll find him, too, if he's still around."

"No telling where he is. Maybe he's in Florida by this time, wondering if he dare take a chance and spend more of his hot money." Bill glanced at Joey from the corner of his eye. "By the way," he continued casually, "who's that fellow Red Baker that's staying at your place?"

"I don't know," Joey answered sharply. "He's leaving today."

"The reason I asked — I met him on the road this morning on my way out here. We stopped and introduced ourselves. He had a pair of binoculars. What is he, a naturalist or something like that?"

"I said I don't know!" Joey's face was flushed, and his voice was shrill. "I don't know anything about him, and I don't want to!"

The warden raised his eyebrows, surprised by the vehemence of the outburst. "I'm sorry — didn't mean to upset you."

Joey wanted to get away before the man asked any more questions. "Look, Warden," he said uneasily, "I've got to go and water Fury. There's a spring up there in the woods on the tote road that leads to Pine Ridge. Do you mind if I ride up and let him drink?"

"No, go right ahead. As a matter of fact, I was about to suggest that you go up and check that area. My men are patrolling farther to the north, and I'd like you to go to the ridge and look around. This wind has got me plenty worried."

"Okay. If I see anybody in the woods, I'll tell them you said they had to get out."

"Fine, that's the idea." The warden held Fury's bridle while Joey mounted. "Son," he said earnestly, when Joey was seated, "please don't leave the valley. I don't know where you were going when I stopped you, but I'm glad I did, because I need you." He looked up into Joey's clouded face. "Jim needs you, too." Joey closed his eyes and looked away. Bill slapped him on the leg. "Good luck, ranger; keep your eyes peeled."

Joey brought his knees in and turned Fury south toward the tote road. He was trying not to think of Jim and the Broken Wheel, but it was hard to get them out of his mind.

After Mr. Barstow and David had been turned back from the check point, they rode in embarrassed silence until they reached the gate of their ranch. Before turning in, Barstow stopped the car and looked around at his son. "Well, David," he said sorrowfully, "our day together has been ruined."

"I'm sorry, Dad," the boy murmured. "I know you gave up a lot to take me hunting, but maybe we can go next week."

"I wanted you to go today." He motioned to the wicker basket in the back seat. "The cook packed a fine lunch, and we would've had a good time." A note of anger crept into his voice. "If it hadn't been for that fool warden, you might be shooting a deer this very minute."

"But, Dad," David argued feebly, "I think the warden was right. *Nobody's* allowed to hunt today on account of the danger of fire."

His father took him gently by the arm. "What's the matter — don't you trust your old dad to know his way around the woods?"

"Yes, sir, it isn't that. It's just that we shouldn't go. If we did we'd be breaking the law."

Barstow chuckled. "David, in this life everybody breaks the law now and then — when the law doesn't make sense." He glanced up toward the timberland and made a sudden decision. "By golly, there's deer up there, and I'm going to let you bag one." He turned the car away from the ranch gate and headed up the narrow tote road.

David was alarmed. "Dad! Where are we going?"

"This is a free country," his father answered with a laugh. "We're going to have our picnic, and we're going to get you a deer, and nobody can stop us."

"No — I don't want to go! Let's turn back — *please!*"

"Not a chance. Just leave it to your dad—he knows what he's doing."

David sighed and stared straight ahead as they left the flatland and began the climb up the tree-bordered road. As they rounded a turn, a deer bounded from the woods just ahead of them and dashed across the road into a small clearing. Barstow jammed on the brakes. "Get him, David! Hurry!" He reached into the back seat and handed the boy his rifle. "Shoot! Shoot!" he cried.

While his father steadied him with both arms, David stood up in the car and raised the gun to his shoulder. The animal was a young buck with five-inch prongs, and as the boy took aim he saw its snow-white tail and rump bouncing through the trees just beyond the clearing.

"Shoot, David, shoot!" Barstow commanded.

The boy bit his lip and pulled the trigger. The slug screamed through the branches, many feet above the buck's head. As the echo of the shot died away, a few leaves floated down into the still forest.

"You missed him," his father said, disappointed.

David settled back into his seat. "Yes, sir — I'm sorry."

His father's eyes gleamed. "I wish I'd taken that shot. I wouldn't have missed him." He released the brake, and the car started forward. "Oh, well, we're bound to see another one before lunchtime, so don't worry."

"I'm not worried about not getting the deer." He looked up with wide, pleading eyes. "Dad — please can't we go home?"

"No, sir-ee — not before you bag yourself a deer." He noticed the boy's despairing face. "Come on, son, don't look so glum. I want you to enjoy this outing."

"Yes sir," David said, "I'll try."

As they drove along the tote road, climbing higher and higher, Barstow kept a sharp watch for another deer, but none was to be seen. For several hours they drove back and forth along the summit of Pine

Ridge, and shortly after eleven, David announced that he was hungry.

"So am I," his father said. "We'll drive down to where we saw the deer and have lunch in the clearing. If he's still around, you might get another shot at him."

He drove to a small turnaround and started back. When they arrived at the clearing, he stopped the car, and they both got out. "I'll take the rifles," Barstow said. "You bring the lunch basket." He strode into the clearing and propped the weapons against a rock. "Oh, one more thing," he shouted over his shoulder. "Bring that newspaper from the back seat."

"What do you want this paper for?" David asked as he joined his father.

"To start a fire with. We're going to cook hot dogs."

"But, Dad," the boy said in dismay, "we can't start a fire — it's too dangerous."

"David," his father said almost sharply, "I don't want to hear any more of that foolish talk. Now, while I start the fire, you cut two green sticks to cook the hot dogs on." As he was gathering some sticks of dead wood which lay close at hand, a gust of wind lifted the newspaper and scattered the pages in all directions. After he had recaptured a few sheets he balled them up, piled the kindling over them and struck a match. The flames leaped several feet into the air, then settled down to devour the dry tinder.

"Dad!" David cried. "Be careful!"

His father silenced him with a reproachful look and tossed a few more chunks onto the fire. A few minutes later they were cooking their franks over the glowing coals. Barstow looked at David and smiled.

"If you'd only bagged that deer, I'd be fixing you a real barbecue instead of hot dogs."

"That would've been fine," David said in a low voice.

After they had eaten the franks and the rest of the lunch that had been packed in the basket, they sat in the shade of a cedar and watched the dying fire. "Ah, son, this is really the life," Barstow said, patting his paunch. "A good lunch and a nice rest under the trees. Nothing like it in the world."

David was eyeing the fire with some anxiety. "That's right, Dad, but now I think we'd better put the fire out and start home."

His father sighed and grunted to his feet. "Okay, if that's the way you want it — you're the boss today." He gathered the paper plates and cups and tossed them onto the fire. As they ignited, the updraft caught them and flung flaming scraps into the air.

"Look out!" David shouted. He pursued the glowing bits as they came down, and stomped them out.

A sudden sound on the road caused them to turn their heads. With a quick motion, Barstow tossed David his rifle and snatched up his own.

"Maybe it's the deer!" he whispered tensely. "Be ready!"

The sound on the road now became the recognizable beating of a horse's hoofs. In a moment the rider came into view around the bend.

"It's Joey!" David cried delightedly.

Joey took in the situation at a glance and was horrified. "Put that fire out!" he yelled. "Hurry!"

Barstow shook his head in disgust as Joey leaped from Fury's back and raced to the small blaze.

"You heard the warden!" Joey cried angrily, as he kicked dirt onto the fire. "He told you not to go hunting, and building this fire was a crazy thing to do! Help me, David — we've got to cover this with dirt!"

David glanced anxiously at his father, then hastened to Joey's side.

"Come back here, David!" his father commanded. The boy looked around, fearfully. "At once, David! Come back and get in the car!"

The boy hung his head and walked slowly to the car. After he had taken his seat, his father slid in behind the wheel and started the motor.

Joey shouted without looking around. "Wait! We've got to put this fire out!"

"Put it out yourself!" Barstow shouted. He backed the car into the clearing, turned the wheel violently, and sped up the hill.

Fury pranced nervously to Joey's side. Joey, with his back to the road, was scooping dirt onto the fire with his hands. "Gosh, Fury, that Mr. Barstow oughta be reported. One little spark could burn down this whole forest. It could ruin the range down below, too, if the brush caught fire." He stood up. "Anyway, I'm glad we came along when we did. At least Mr. Barstow has quit hunting and gone back to his ranch." He circled the mound of dirt, making certain that the last ember was dead. When he was satisfied that the danger was over, he vaulted into the saddle and rode from the clearing. The dust that had been raised by Barstow's car was just settling down on the road above. With a gasp, he realized that Barstow hadn't gone back to his ranch at all. Despite the warning, he had driven up the hill instead of down. Joey slapped his rein sharply, and Fury began the long climb to the Pine Ridge road.

Chapter 14
THE INFERNO

Mr. Barstow was boiling with inward rage as he drove the car up the tote road. "I've had my fill of those Newtons," he mumbled, "Jim and Joey both."

David turned and looked up at his father's indignant face. "What'd you say, Dad?"

Barstow forced a smile. "I was just wondering where I might find you a deer."

"But I don't *want* a deer!" David cried sharply. "I want to go home — *now!*" It was the first time he had ever spoken to his father with anything but complete respect, but he wasn't disturbed by his audacity. He knew that his father was wrong and suspected that his father knew it, too, but was blundering ahead just to show him that he wasn't going to allow anybody to push him around.

Barstow had turned pale — his son's angry tone

had shocked him beyond measure. As he was considering how to chastise the boy — something he had never had to do before — he rounded a turn in the road and gave a cry of amazement. A doe was standing in the center of the road, staring straight at the onrushing car. Her nostrils were dilated, her ears erect, as she stood frozen to the spot. As the wheels locked and the tires crunched to a stop on the gravel, the doe turned and leaped in a graceful arc into the woods.

"Now!" Barstow shouted. "Now's your chance!" He thrust David's rifle into his hands, but the boy held it limply and remained seated. "Okay," the man cried n exasperation, "if you don't shoot, ' will!" He snatched up his own gun and fired at the retreating animal.

"You missed her," David said quietly.

The doc's white flag was just disappearing among the trees as Barstow fired another shot. He opened the door and sprang from the car. "I may have hit her that time!" he shouted excitedly.

"I don't think so," the boy said, in the same quiet voice.

Barstow was annoyed by his son's negative attitude. "Well, if I did hit her she won't get very far. Come on, we're going to follow her."

With a sigh, David stepped from the car and joined his father at the edge of the road.

"You forgot your gun," his father said. "Go back and get it."

As David turned back to the car, Barstow reached nervously for a cigarette, lighted it, and ground the charred match into the gravel with his hunting boot. He took two deep puffs while David was getting his gun. "Hurry up," he called, "before she gets too far away."

The boy picked the weapon up from the front seat and rejoined his father. "Okay, Dad," he said listlessly, "let's go."

Barstow pushed him forward. "You lead the way, son, I want this deer to be yours."

David parted the bushes and stepped into the woods. His father followed a few paces behind him, the cigarette dangling from his lips. After they had progressed several hundred feet, David stopped. "I think she got away," he called back over his shoulder.

"We're certainly not going to give up now. Keep going." Barstow took a few more puffs on the cigarette and tossed it carelessly away.

As the hunters plunged more deeply into the thicket, a small gust of wind rolled the cigarette onto a patch of dry grass. Almost instantly, a slender, brown wisp began to glow, and a tiny spiral of smoke drifted lazily upward. Another gust picked up the dead debris of the forest floor, and a handful of dry leaves were blown onto the patch of glowing grass, then lifted, flaming, into the air by the hot draft of the blaze. Like giant fireflies, they floated through the disturbed air and came to rest in the underbrush at the foot of a small, dead pine. As the dry pile ignited, the yellow tongues shot upward and the pine crackled into flame, like a discarded Christmas tree that had been set afire by mischievous boys. A hundred yards up the slope, Barstow was still hunting stubbornly for David's deer.

Joey heard the two rifle shots when he was still half a mile down the road. Fury threw his ears forward and broke into a gallop. When they arrived at the parked automobile, Joey saw bootprints in the dust and turned Fury into the woods.

"That Mr. Barstow must be crazy," he muttered. "If he isn't, why would he — " He ended in midsentence, as Fury jerked his head up and neighed warningly. It was a peculiar sound that Joey had never heard before — a strange combination of urgency and fear. As Fury slowed down and sniffed apprehensively, Joey felt a tremor run through the stallion's body. "What is it? What's the matter?" Fury gave a low whinny and twisted his head backward. Joey saw the white of one frightened eye. He leaned forward and peered through the dark lane of trees. A sudden rush of wind brought a gray cloud from the depths of the thicket. Its odor was familiar and terrifying. "Smoke," Joey whispered in alarm.

He urged Fury forward, thinking angrily that Barstow had built another campfire. Before he learned the truth, he heard a crisp crackling in the brush and saw a tongue of flame shoot up into the limbs of a huge pine. Joey was terrified at the sight. He had no fear for his own safety just yet. He thought only of the terrible consequences to the ridge if the fire were to spread. Both he and Fury were coughing now as the smoke grew thicker. At the perimeter of the fire, he slid to the ground and attempted to extinguish a small blaze which had started to devour a pile of last autumn's fallen leaves. There was no loose dirt to throw on the flames — the ground was a mass of tangled roots. Realizing that stomping would do no good at all, he looked up at the pine which had now become a blazing torch. He knew that it was no longer a surface fire fed by ground litter and small growth. It was threatening to become a crown fire — the most dreaded fire of all.

Joey had learned from Warden Gibson's lectures that a crown fire is caused by wind-blown sparks and embers which ignite the upper limbs of the tallest trees. Carried by the wind overhead, the eager flames reach out to the tops of other trees, starting numerous fires in addition to the original one, which by itself might have been fought and conquered if isolated in time.

Other pines were flaming now, their sap boiling and crackling. Fury gave a cry of pain as a live ember fell upon his rump. Joey brushed it off with his hand and snatched the bridle to stop Fury from bucking. Suddenly he thought of the Barstows and gave a horrified gasp as he realized that they would be trapped unless he found them and led them out. Vaulting into the saddle, he rode around the fire in a wide circle, and when he reached the opposite side, he plunged deeper into the forest, calling their names.

On Lost Hill Tower, Ranger Thompson was sweeping the 360 degrees of the horizon with his binoculars. As he swung the glasses slowly to the north his body tensed suddenly. Instinctively he reached for the radio panel and flipped the switch. "Lost Hill Tower to all units!" he cried urgently into the mike. . . . "Lost Hill Tower to all units! . . . Listen and get it clear! Fire has broken out on Pine Ridge! . . . Repeat — fire has broken out on Pine Ridge! All men and equipment report to the area at once!" He closed the switch and raised his glasses toward Pine Ridge. A thin column of smoke was rising into the air and creeping slowly eastward. Presently, a wave of flame shot up, and when the wind caught it a second flame appeared in the neighboring treetops.

The loudspeaker crackled. "K-S-M to Lost Hill Tower. . . . Thompson, do you hear me?"

"Yes, come in, Bill."

"How bad is it?"

"Real bad — looks like a crown."

"Can you pinpoint it?"

"Almost. About a mile up from the Barstow ranch right off the tote road."

Thompson heard the warden's sharp intake of breath. "What's the matter, Bill?"

"Joey Newton's up there! He's patrolling the ridge!"

"You sure?"

"*Yes* — I sent him!" The warden's voice became shrill and commanding. "Contact HQ. . . . Tell them to phone Jim Newton at the BW. . . . Tell him you think Joey's in the fire area. . . . Repeat — you *think* he's there — don't make it definite — we don't want to scare Newton stiff. . . . Tell him to drive up and meet me at the tote road. Got that straight?"

"Roger."

"Okay, I'm headed there now. Keep in touch — out!"

Thompson relayed the message to HQ, and Jim had the news almost at once. A moment later, the station wagon roared through the gate of the BW, carrying Jim, Pete, and Red Baker toward the big burn.

David Barstow stopped under a pine tree and walked back to his father, who had slowed down considerably and fallen twenty yards behind. "Dad," he said wearily, "I'm tired — I want to go home."

The puffing man welcomed the suggestion without admitting it. "Okay, David; if that's the way you feel, we'll start back." He peered through the trees and shook his head. "Too bad we didn't catch up to that doe. I was sure my last shot winged her a little."

They turned and retraced their steps through the dense growth. After they had covered a quarter of a mile Barstow began to cough violently. "What's the matter?" David asked.

"I don't know, my throat burns."

David noticed that his father's eyes were watering. He too had noticed a peculiar sensation in his throat. He looked upward and saw that the patch of daylight was dimmed by a thin, gray cloud. "Dad," he said anxiously, "that's smoke."

Barstow dabbed at his eyes and glanced up. "You're right, I smell it." As they continued down the sloping terrain, the dark shadows of the forest became tinted with a pink glow.

"What's that funny light?" David asked.

His father's eyes widened. "It — it looks like fire."

As they came to a small clearing, a handful of embers shot up through the tall trees directly ahead of them.

"It *is* fire!" David cried. "The woods are on fire!"

Horrified, Barstow's hand shot up to his breast pocket and felt the package of cigarettes. As he remembered the half-smoked butt that he had thrown away, he knew clearly what had happened. "We've got to get to the car!" he announced in a strangled voice. "Come on, run! Stay close to me!"

They dropped their rifles and ran forward, but as they reached the opposite edge of the clearing, a wall of flame shot up before them and turned them away. They shielded their eyes with their arms and stepped backward.

"The fire's between us and the car!" David shouted. "What'll we do?"

His father coughed and pointed to the left. "We've got to go around it! Hold your handkerchief to your mouth and follow me!"

As they ran toward the unburned area, a great cedar caught fire in its low branches and showered them with sparks. In terror, they reversed their direction. The branches in their path were heavily interlaced, and Barstow clawed at them furiously before he found an opening. "Stay close behind me!" he called hoarsely. "Don't let's get separated!"

As they fought their way slowly through the thicket, the wind-whipped flames swept over the topmost branches, and it seemed as though they were standing under a blazing tent. Falling sparks came to rest on their clothing, and they flicked them off with their handkerchiefs. As a giant pine exploded, a sudden billow of smoke engulfed them and David threw his hands over his eyes. As he moved forward, unable to see, he stumbled over a rotted log and fell to the ground. Unaware that David was no longer close behind him, Barstow pushed ahead. A moment later he heard the boy's faint voice in the distance. "Dad, where are you? *Dad!*"

Barstow whirled, realizing for the first time that his son was not following at his heels. "David!" he called in dismay. "David — I'm over here!" Receiving no answer, he started back. He had taken but a few steps when a massive limb, alive with fire, crashed at his feet. He fell back momentarily, and as he attempted to step around the flaming limb the underbrush ignited in a quick burst, and his path of rescue was cut off. "David!" he cried in horror. "David — answer me!"

It was impossible for him to know whether David answered or not. No human voice could be heard above the thunderous roar of the inferno.

Fury was crashing through the underbrush at the rim of the fire. Joey lay flat against the black mane, calling for the Barstows at the top of his voice. When a falling ember ignited a dead bush, Fury leaped back in fear, almost throwing Joey from the saddle.

"Easy, Fury, easy!" Joey shouted. "We'll get out of this, but we've got to find them first!" Fury turned his body halfway around and danced sideways, like a scurrying crab. "I know you're scared, Fury — I am, too! The wind's blowing the fire all around; the whole ridge is burning!" Hearing a sharp crack overhead, he slapped Fury on the neck, and the horse sprang forward just in time to avoid another limb which came hissing earthward. Joey shuddered. It had been a near miss.

As they pressed forward in a wide arc, Fury rose suddenly to his hind legs. He had come face to face with a deer which had been dashing blindly through the smoke. The deer stopped short and looked at Fury with dilated eyes, then turned in terror and darted straight toward the heart of the fire.

"Oh, no!" Joey moaned helplessly. "Not that way!"

The animal made a sudden turn to its left, and for a moment stood silhouetted against a high wall of flame. Its head went up as it sniffed in several directions, then, to Joey's relief, it bounded across a strip of blackened grass and disappeared into the unburned thicket.

Joey urged Fury into a wider circle, calling frantically for the Barstows. His eyes were filled with smoke tears, and Fury had become almost unmanageable. In the dense, hot cloud which enveloped them, breathing had become difficult, and soon Joey came to the sickening realization that he would have to abandon the search and seek his own safety. He jerked the rein violently and turned Fury northward, hoping to reach a section of the tote road that had not yet been overrun by fire. As Fury pounded into a small clearing, Joey saw something glistening on the ground — a rifle! Five feet beyond it lay a second rifle. He cupped his hand and called, "Mr. Barstow! . . . David!" He listened, but there was no reply. Nothing could be heard in the smoke-filled clearing but the ominous crackle of flames and the crash of falling trees.

Suddenly, in a shifting wind, the fire bore down directly upon Joey. Clouds of smoke and embers rolled in like a wave. He gasped in an effort to find air to breathe, and Fury wheezed and snorted like an engine. When the woods behind them burst into flame, Joey fell forward and encircled Fury's neck with his arms. In his despair he remembered what Warden Gibson had told him that morning at the check point: "Nobody knows how terrifying it is to be caught in the middle of a burning forest until he's actually had the experience. Then, sometimes, it's too late." He buried his face in the black mane and wished that he could see Jim again — just once more.

Chapter 15
ENTER MIKE DRISCOLL

Opposite the gate of the Barstow ranch, where the tote road to the ridge began, Firewarden Bill Gibson set up his base of operations. Rangers and volunteers were pouring into the intersection from all directions. The fire on Pine Ridge had alerted every rancher and wrangler in the valley, and each man knew that his strong arms and back would be needed if a major catastrophe was to be avoided.

A truckload of Barstow's cowhands, being closest to the fire, had been the first on the scene. Armed with hoes, axes, and chain saws, they had driven up the road to fight the fire even before Bill Gibson arrived on the scene from the check point.

As Bill braked his car and leaped out, Chick Lacy and the men of his jeep crew came speeding through the gate of the Barstow ranch. Chick stopped the jeep and climbed out lazily.

197

"Hi, Warden," he drawled, with a lopsided grin. "What's new?"

Bill was in no mood to appreciate the man's ill-timed attempt at humor. "I could use volunteers," he said sharply. "If you men want to help, drive up there and start cutting a firebreak." He glanced to the north. "My rangers will be coming down any minute to work with you."

One of Chick's men spoke up. "What about startin' a couple of backfires?"

The warden shook his head. "Backfires are dangerous. If the wind shifts you could find yourselves trapped. If backfires become necessary I'll radio the order to my men."

Chick Lacy looked up at the smoke-blackened sky. High overhead, the steady west wind was carrying flaming embers toward the Barstow ranch, and bits of charred debris were already falling on the road. Chick spat out a matchstick. "I'd say Barstow's layout's a mite too close to the fire, wouldn't you?"

Bill nodded. "Unless we get the burn under control in record time, that ranch is going to burn up. By the way, Lacy, where *is* Barstow?"

Chick shrugged. "Don't ask me."

One of the men called out from the jeep. "The boss went huntin' this mornin' with his kid."

Bill whirled angrily. "But I turned them back! Aren't they in the ranch house?"

"Nope. I hollered for 'em when I first seen the fire, but didn't git no answer."

"Well, if they're up on Pine Ridge they're in danger of being burned alive. Get up there in a hurry and look for them. Spread the word."

Chick Lacy hesitated, looking back uncertainly toward the bunkhouse. "Mebbe I oughta look after the ranch."

"Forget it! Their lives are more important than their ranch, so get going!"

With another anxious glance at the bunkhouse, Chick eased back into the jeep and headed up the tote road. Fire fighters were arriving in great numbers, and as each truckload checked in, the warden gave them instructions and sent them on their way. A quarter of an hour after a bulldozer had been dispatched to the blaze, the station wagon from the Broken Wheel roared onto the scene. Jim's face was ashen as he pulled up beside the warden's car.

"Bill! Any word about Joey?"

"Not yet, Jim."

Jim leaped out. "Your HQ phoned and said he might be up on Pine Ridge! Whose idea was that?"

"Mine."

Jim grabbed the man by the shoulder. "Well, is he there, or isn't he?"

"He is."

"How do you know?"

Bill drew a deep breath. "Because I sent him up on fire patrol."

Jim groaned and looked toward the flaming ridge. Pete and Red Baker had come from the car to stand beside him.

"Easy, Jim," Pete muttered. "Mebbe Joey got out on the other side."

Jim pushed between Pete and Red and darted for the station wagon.

"Hold it!" the warden shouted. "You can't get that car up there! The road's clogged with trucks and tractors!"

Jim's broad shoulders sagged. "Okay, what *can* I do? Suppose you tell me!"

Gibson took his arm. "I've got to give it to you straight, Jim. It's too late now to *start* looking for Joey. The blaze is spread over too great an area. The men who got up there first are the only ones who could possibly have gotten him out."

Jim turned away, pounding his fists together in frustration. Pete stared at the ground, his wrinkled face looking ten years older. Red Baker spoke to the warden in a low voice.

"What do you think Joey's chances are?"

"Between you and me, not very good."

Red looked at the Barstow Ranch. The entire layout was enveloped in smoke. "I don't see any action at Barstow's, Warden. Everybody gone?" Bill nodded. "What about that fellow Chick Lacy? Have you seen *him*?"

"Yes, he's up at the burn, looking for Barstow and his son. I have a hunch they're in danger, too."

Jim overheard the remark and swung around. "What's that? You say Barstow and David are up there?"

"I'm not sure, Jim, but they went hunting against my orders. It's just possible that they went up to the ridge."

A sudden roar of voices on the hillside caused

them to look up. The men who were cutting a fire-break at the first turn of the tote road were calling and gesticulating. A stout man with a smoke-blackened face was running down past them toward the main highway.

Pete pointed in amazement. "Look! Ain't that Barstow?"

They recognized the man as he came nearer. It was Barstow, in a feverish state of fear and exhaustion. His eyebrows were singed, and his clothing was scorched in many places.

"David — my son! Save David! He's up there — in the fire." Great sobs rose from his throat, and his face was racked with pain. He sank wearily to the ground. "It's all my fault! You told me not to go, but I was a fool!"

Gibson took him firmly by the shoulders. "Barstow — did *you* start that fire?"

"I didn't mean to. . . . There was a deer . . . I had a cigarette . . . I — I threw it away and — "

Jim lunged forward and yanked the man to his feet. "You *what?*" His right fist was clenched as he glared into Barstow's face.

Pete and the warden sprang to Jim's side and pulled him away.

"Hold it, Jim!" Gibson commanded.

Jim pointed accusingly at Barstow. "But you heard what he said! If it hadn't been for him, Joey would — "

"I know that!" the warden cut in. "But leave him alone! Look at him — he's paying for what he's done."

"He shore is," Pete muttered, "an' so help me, I pity him."

Jim glanced at the despairing man, then shook his head and turned away. Barstow was pounding the warden's car with his fist.

"It's my fault," he groaned, "my fault . . ."

As a billow of hot smoke bore down upon the group, Barstow buried his face in his arms and wept.

Panic stricken and fighting for breath, David Barstow had stumbled from one burning thicket to another, calling for his father. As the smoke swirled about him, and no sound was to be heard but the roar and crackle of the blaze, he realized that he would have to find his way out alone. Suddenly there was an ominous crash far above his head, and he threw up his arms for protection as smoking limbs and branches fell all around him. One of the branches knocked him to the ground, and as he pushed it away and tried to rise, he felt a sharp pain in his ankle. In horror he saw that his leg had been pinned beneath a heavy log. Whimpering with pain and fright he tried to wrench his leg free, but the log was too heavy and the slightest movement was agony. He called again for his father, and as he tried once more to free his leg the entire forest seemed to revolve in a gray mist, and he lost consciousness.

Sometimes, when a crown fire leaps the treetops, an upward gust of wind will carry the flames over one area without touching it, thus leaving an unburned patch beneath. It was in such a pocket that David was trapped, and into which pure chance brought Joey and Fury.

As Joey entered the untouched area he looked around hopefully. The wind had carried the fire in front of him, and there seemed to be less danger for the moment, as long as no embers fell.

"Fury!" he cried. "Maybe we're going to make it!"

Fury snorted and pawed the ground. As Joey looked upward at the black silhouettes of burned trees around the rim of the circle, Fury took several steps forward and sniffed at a pile of fallen branches.

"What is it, Fury?" Joey shouted. A sudden movement among the branches caused him to cry out in surprise. He slid from his saddle and pulled the branches aside, thinking that he would find a trapped animal. To his amazement, he discovered that it was David Barstow.

"David! Are you all right?"

The boy was just recovering consciousness. "I'm caught," he moaned. "It's my leg."

"Hold still — I'll try to get you out." Joey tugged at the heavy log but it was too much for his strength. A shower of sparks fell among the dead branches, setting them afire. He kicked them away, and as the ground litter burst into flame he knew that he was in danger again and would have to work fast to save David. "Fury!" he cried. "Come help me!"

Fury had backed away from the blazing underbrush, but now he responded obediently to Joey's urgent call. Joey reached for his lariat and tied it to the saddle horn. Casting the free end over a stout branch above David's head, he fastened the dangling rope to the log. "Now, Fury," he called, "back up!"

The stallion backed away, and as the log lifted,

Joey dragged David out from under it. "We've got to hurry! Can you stand up?"

The boy tried to rise but fell back, groaning with pain. "I can't make it — it hurts something awful."

Joey bent down. "Put your arm around my shoulders."

With Joey's help, David finally stood upright, but the injured leg was unable to bear his weight. "Where's Dad?" he moaned. "Have you seen my dad?"

"No, but maybe he got out all right." Joey glanced at the approaching ground flames as he jerked the rope from the saddle horn. There wasn't a second to lose. "If *we're* going to get out, we've got to get you on Fury's back." He called to Fury. "Kneel down, Fury! . . . Come on — get down! . . . *Down!*"

Fury looked uncertainly at the advancing flames and lowered himself to the ground. Joey flung his leg over the broad rump and helped David into the saddle.

"Okay, Fury — get up!"

As Fury rose to his feet with his double burden, a small evergreen burst into flames at his heels, and he shot forward like an arrow from a bow. With his bridle hanging free, he galloped along a narrow corridor of blackened waste, bordered by blazing trees. Guided by instinct, he raced across the wind, parallel to the fire. Following a great, downward-sloping circle at the fire's edge, he crashed through the smoking forest until he finally reached the firebreak near the lower end of the tote road.

The toiling men cheered as the great stallion

broke into the open and thundered past the chugging tractors. As the glad cries arose all down the line, the group at the warden's car looked up through the billowing smoke.

"It's *Joey!*" Jim cried. "*Joey! Joey!*"

"Thank goodness," Pete said quietly. "He's got David, too."

The warden hung up his microphone and tapped Barstow on the shoulder. "Take a look — here comes your boy."

Barstow lifted his head from his arms. "What? What did you say?"

Bill Gibson pointed. Jim had just taken Fury's bridle. Barstow gave a joyous cry and staggered forward.

As Joey jumped to the ground, Jim gathered him tenderly in his arms. "Are you all right, son?"

"Yes, but David's hurt. It's his leg."

Red Baker lifted the injured boy from the saddle.

David saw his father coming toward him. "*Dad —* you got out! You're *safe!*"

Barstow nodded and clutched the boy to his chest.

"Joey saved my life! I was trapped in the fire and he saved my life!"

Barstow reached out and placed his hand tenderly against Joey's cheek. "Thank you," he muttered hoarsely. "By saving David's life, you saved mine, too. You're a very brave boy."

"It wasn't really me," Joey said, "it was Fury. Without Fury, we wouldn't have gotten out at all."

A sharp exclamation from the warden brought all heads around at once. He was pointing to Barstow's ranch house. The roof was burning fiercely, and tongues of flame were licking at the upstairs windows. Bales of hay stacked along the barn were smoking, and the wind was blowing embers toward the bunkhouse.

"Come on!" Jim shouted. "Let's see what we can save!"

He dashed through the gate, followed by Pete and Red Baker. Joey jumped on Fury's back and rode after them.

Barstow was kneeling on the ground, examining David's injured leg. He looked up and called, "Don't bother about my place! As long as our boys are safe, I don't care if the ranch burns to the ground!"

Even before the group arrived at the flaming house, they knew that nothing could be done. The ground floor had caught fire, and the entire building was doomed.

"Mebbe we can save the stock in the barn!" Pete yelled. "Let's try!"

"The thing to do," Jim shouted, "is to move those bales away from the wall!"

Aided by Joey and Red Baker, he and Pete began to roll the heavy feed bales into the driveway. While they were laboring, Chick Lacy roared up the driveway in his jeep and sped past them, narrowly missing Fury. Fury jumped backward and gave a startled neigh.

"Hey!" Joey called angrily. "Watch where you're going!"

Chick stopped the jeep near the door of the bunkhouse and dashed inside. Red Baker straightened up and spoke softly to Jim.

"I think this is it! Keep Joey here."

"Right!" Jim said. He raised his voice. "Joey, give me a hand with this bale."

"Okay." As Joey strained at one end of the heavy load, he looked back over his shoulder and saw Red disappearing behind the barn, moving stealthily. Joey frowned. "Jim, where's Red going?"

Jim hesitated for a second. "Why — uh — he wants to check the bunkhouse to see if it can be saved."

"Oh." Since his close brush with death in the woods, Joey had not given much thought to his troubles at the Broken Wheel. Now the bitter memory of his disappointment rushed back, and he attacked the bale fiercely in an effort to erase it from his mind.

Behind the barn, Red Baker patted the bulge in his pocket and crouched low as he loped toward the bunkhouse. Small flames were rising from its roof. Moving furtively through the tall grass, he came up behind the long, low building and peered through the back window. In the dancing light cast by the blaze at the main house, he saw Chick Lacy desperately ripping up the floor boards with a claw hammer. Red smiled grimly and ran around to the front of the building. When he reached the jeep, he bent low so as not to be seen from the doorway; quickly his hand shot up and snatched the key from the ignition. Dropping the key in his pocket, he returned to the back window. As Red watched, Chick Lacy lifted a heavy suitcase from the hole in the floor and carried it to the door. With a cautious glance toward the barn, he dashed out to the jeep and dumped the suitcase onto the seat. Leaping in behind the wheel, he reached for the key and found it gone. With a cry of anger he searched wildly for it on the floor. When he didn't find it he glanced fearfully down the driveway, snatched the suitcase, and leaped to the ground. As he started running toward the barn, a sharp command rang out behind his back.

"Kislake! *Freeze!*"

Chick spun around. Red Baker stood beside the jeep, pointing his automatic. Chick's jaw fell, and his face lengthened into an expression of utter disbelief.

"Drop the suitcase!" Red barked. "*Drop* it!"

Chick twisted his body and looked toward the barn, considering his chances. Joey and Fury stood in the way of his escape, but there were a number of cars parked near the ranch gate, and he decided to make a run for one of them. As he whirled and dashed down the driveway, Red fired a shot over his head.

At the crack of the automatic, Fury jerked his head up and began a nervous dance. Joey ran to him, attempting to catch hold of his bridle. From the corner of his eye he saw Chick coming toward him, pursued by Red Baker.

"Joey!" Red cried. "Get back!"

Joey saw the gun in Red's hand, and gasped in amazement. Jim and Pete were in the smoking hayloft, looking down.

"Get back, Joey!" Jim shouted. "Get back!"

Chick was now only a few feet from Joey, and Red was unable to chance another shot. A second later, Chick bore down on Joey and knocked him to the ground with his fist. As Joey fell heavily into the dust, Fury gave a whistle of rage and rose to his hind legs in the fighting stance of the stallion. His forelegs raked the air, close to Chick's face. Chick dropped the suitcase and backed into the bales of hay.

"Git him off!" he screamed. "Git him away!"

As Red Baker arrived, Fury had the cowering man cornered among the bales. "Okay, Joey," Red directed, "call Fury off."

Jim and Pete had slid down the loading rope. Joey turned to Jim, a perplexed look on his face.

"Do as he says!" Jim cried. "Call him off!"

Joey grabbed Fury's bridle and pulled him away from the shrieking Lacy. Red Baker moved in quickly with a pair of handcuffs and chained Lacy to an iron pipe on the water trough.

"Good work, Mike," Jim said. "You've got your man."

Red grinned. "Correction — *Fury* got my man."

Joey spoke to Jim, completely bewildered. "Jim — this is *Red*. You called him Mike."

"Danged if you didn't," Pete muttered. "How come you called him Mike all of a sudden?"

Jim wiped his brow. "You tell them, Mike."

Red drew a small, black case from his pocket and handed it to Joey, who opened it with Pete staring over his shoulder. The contents of the case told them that Red Baker was Mike Driscoll of the FBI.

Joey was too dumbfounded to speak. It was Pete who found his voice first.

"Wal, Mike, now we know who *you* are, but how come you put bracelets on this Lacy critter?"

"Another correction," Mike said. "*His* real name is Harry Kislake. Right, Kislake?"

"Drop dead!" his glowering prisoner grunted.

Mike Driscoll bent down and unfastened the lock on the suitcase. "Brace yourselves for a shock, men." As he flipped the lid open, Joey and the others found themselves staring down at packages of bright green bank notes.

"Jumpin' Jee — hoshaphat!" Pete exclaimed.

Mike laughed. "You said it. Eighty thousand dollars, less the ten that Kislake spent at Matt Castle's store."

A jagged flash of lightning rent the air, followed by a cannonade of thunderclaps. Almost before Mike could close the suitcase, the clouds ripped open and heavy sheets of rain swept over the valley, carried forward by a cool wind. A mighty cheer went up from the fire fighters on the tote road.

Giant drops were falling upon Fury's steaming back and trickling down his legs. He raised his head skyward, closed his eyes, and whinnied with delight.

Chapter 16
FURY TAKES A BOW

There was no time for the further explanations that Joey was dying to hear. A moment after the storm broke, the hayloft burst into flame, and Jim and Pete dashed into the ground floor of the barn to bring out the terrified horses.

"Joey," Jim called back over his shoulder, "you ride Fury back to the BW and wait for us. We'll be there as soon as we can."

"Okay, Jim." Joey mounted Fury and set out on his long, wet ride.

A short while later, Mike Driscoll shackled his prisoner to the coatrack in the back seat of a borrowed car and drove him to the town jail. After the stolen money had been locked away in the bank vault, Mike returned to the jail and talked seriously with the police chief for a few hours. When their conversation was over, he started back to the Broken Wheel where at Jim's invitation he was to spend another night.

Shortly before seven in the evening, Warden Gibson announced that the forest fire was under control, and the multitude of toil-worn fighters departed for their homes. Although the greater part of Pine Ridge had been saved, the Barstow ranch lay in ruins.

The blessed rain was still falling steadily as Mike Driscoll drove up the porch of the BW. Joey saw his headlights cutting through the gloom and raced out to meet him with a question.

"Did you have any trouble with Chick Lacy — I mean Harry Kislake?"

"Nope," Mike answered as he ran up the steps. "Kislake's in jail, and the money's in the bank. Are Jim and Pete back yet?"

"Yes, they got in a little while ago. Pete's cooking supper."

"Good, I'm hungry. By the way, what happened to the Barstows? I heard from the police that their ranch was destroyed."

"That's right. Mr. Barstow took David to town to have the doctor look at his leg. Jim invited them to come and live with us for awhile, but they're going to stay at the hotel."

Mike raised an eyebrow. "That was very decent of Jim, after the way Barstow treated him."

Joey smiled. "Well, you know Jim — that's the way he is. Anyway, I think Mr. Barstow's kind of reformed. After David came back alive from the fire, he seemed like a different man."

"I should think so. I imagine he learned quite a

few lessons today. And he owes you a great debt for saving his son's life."

Joey looked fondly toward the barn. "It was Fury — he's the one that got us out. You know what, Mike — I rode him all the way back in the rain and it was swell. After I rubbed him down I took a hot bath, and now I feel wonderful."

Mike clapped him on the shoulder. "I feel wonderful, too, Joey. And before we hit the sack tonight, you and I have a lot to talk about."

Joey looked up with a shy grin. "I guess I acted like a big dope."

"Don't say that. You had a perfect right to act the way you did. We'll hash it over later, okay?"

"Okay, Mike."

They went inside, and soon after Mike had changed into a set of Jim's clothes, Pete announced that supper was ready.

The moment they sat down, Joey begged Mike to tell him all about the Kislake case. Mike started at the beginning.

"Well, as you know, it's a federal offense to rob a Federal bank, so that's how the FBI came into the picture. The police in Helena, Montana, sent us the fingerprints of the robber who escaped. They belonged to a man named Harry Kislake, who had a criminal record, so we knew that Kislake was the man we had to hunt for. Copies of his picture were sent to FBI agents all over the country, and we memorized his features so that we'd know him if we ever ran across him."

"Ya'd never fergit a face like his," Pete growled. "He looks like the underside of a hyena."

Mike chuckled. "Anyway, when the ten-dollar bill from the bank loot turned up at Matt Castle's, I was sent out here as a character named Red Baker to look for Kislake. Before I came to the Broken Wheel I called on a good many ranches, hoping to spot him just by chance. After I got settled here with you, I heard so much about Chick Lacy's villainous behavior I was curious to have a look at him. I got my chance, Joey, the night you and I went to the movie. When the lights came on in the theater, I recognized him immediately as Harry Kislake."

"Wait a second," Joey broke in. "The paper said the robber had light-colored hair. Chick Lacy's hair was black."

"That's right, but when we had our fight on the parking lot I got a good look at him under the bright lights and was pretty sure his hair had been dyed."

"By gosh, you're right," Jim said. "His hair and eyebrows looked much too black for his light eyes and fair skin."

Mike nodded. "He did a bad dye job on himself. He should've gone to a beauty parlor." He paused to eat a few bites of supper, then continued his story. "I wasn't satisfied to identify Kislake by appearance alone. I had to get his fingerprints. The day after the fight, I rode out to the Barstow ranch on the pretense of asking about his health. While I was there, I tossed him a prepared pack of cigarettes and got his prints on the cellophane wrapper. When I got back here, I compared the prints with a set of Kislake's that I'd brought along and knew for sure that Lacy was Kislake."

"Why didn't ya go right back out there an' pinch him?" Pete asked.

"I would have, Pete, but if I'd sent him to jail, maybe we never would've found the stolen money. Today's fire brought the whole thing to a head. When he drove back to the burning bunkhouse in such a hurry, I knew that the loot must be hidden somewhere in the building, and that he was trying to rescue it before it was destroyed." Mike threw up his hands. "Well, that's *my* story." He grinned wryly at Jim. "Now I think Pete and Joey are waiting to hear yours. When you covered for me last night and this morning you sure got yourself into a peck of trouble."

"You can say that again," Jim agreed solemnly. "I almost broke up our happy family."

Joey turned to Jim in surprise. "Jim! Did *you* know that Mike was an FBI man?"

"Not until last night, Joey. Before that, I didn't know any more about him than you and Pete did. But when you told me about seeing him shooting and riding, I made up my mind to accuse him point-blank of being a fake and throw him off the ranch. When he and I went down to the gate for a show-down, I was sore as a boil until he showed me his credentials and told me that he was an FBI agent in disguise. He convinced me that it was absolutely necessary to keep his secret until after he'd make his arrest. If it had leaked out even by accident, Kislake might have escaped." Jim glanced from Pete to Joey. "Well — I played my part, but it almost caused the loss of my two best friends."

"Yer dang right it did," Pete said with an abashed grin. "I was so all-fired mad, I was ready to shove off fer Timbuktu."

"So was I," Joey said in a low voice. "I couldn't understand why you were treating me that way."

Jim sighed. "Well, it's all over, thank goodness. Am I forgiven?"

"Shore," Pete drawled. "Come to think of it, Jim, I bet you suffered more'n me an' Joey put together."

Mike raised his water glass. "And now I'd like to propose a toast — to three of the finest friends I've ever made in my life."

After he had sipped his water, a silence fell over the room, as the members of the Broken Wheel family exchanged warm, appreciative glances. After a moment, Jim cleared his throat.

"We thank you for saying that, Mike — and we want you to know that we're proud to be your friends." He raised his own glass. "And now we'll all drink a toast to you — a fine, courageous man."

Mike Driscoll flushed with pleasure as his companions drank his health.

"Wait a minute!" Joey cried suddenly. "Don't drink it all — there's somebody we almost forgot!" He jumped up from the table. "Come on — bring your glasses."

He walked to the window, followed by the three men.

"To the king of them all!" Joey said, in a soft, loving voice.

As they drained their glasses, the angled outline of the barn loomed up darkly through the slanting rain.

*   *   *

On a crisp, golden day in early October, Mr. Barstow held the biggest barbecue in anybody's memory, on the land where his ranch buildings had stood. Mike Driscoll had come out from Chicago, and all the dwellers of the valley had been asked to attend. The engraved invitations stated that Joey Newton and Fury were to be the guests of honor.

Late in the afternoon, after everyone had eaten his fill and the town band had played a rousing concert of western and patriotic tunes, Mr. Barstow climbed to the platform that had been built on the ruins of his chimney and made a speech into the microphone. It was a brand new Mr. Barstow, whom none of them had ever seen before — a gracious, pleasant, neighborly man. With David standing at his side, he welcomed the crowd and said that he hoped they would return many times, after his new ranch had been built. (*Applause.*) He beamed over the throng and announced that he was donating the latest model fire-fighting apparatus and equipment to the valley for its future protection. (*Greater applause.*) Then, pointing to Jim Newton, whom he called "my good friend and neighbor," he expressed his regret that he had been so short sighted as to cause the capture of the mustangs, and added proudly that he was joining Jim's committee. He also promised to urge the passage of the bill to protect the wild horses that had been introduced in the Congress of the United States. (*Thunderous applause.*)

Now Mr. Barstow requested Joey to mount Fury and ride forward to the front of the crowd. (*Cheers*

217

and whistles.) As Joey sat proudly in the saddle, looking upward, David took the microphone and thanked him and Fury for having saved his life.

Finally, Mike Driscoll was called to the platform. As an expectant hush fell over the assembled ranchers, Mike strummed a few chords on his guitar and announced that instead of making a speech he was going to sing "The Ballad of Fury." Everyone was urged to join in the chorus. After he had sung a verse and chorus alone, the band joined in lustily, and soon the valley was ringing with music.

> FU — RY! . . . . FU — RY!
> From Oregon east to Miss — ou — ri,
> Many fine horses are roaming the land —
> But king of them all is *Fury!*

When the song was ended, and the last echoes of melody had faded on the distant ridge, Joey broke into a wide grin — and Fury took a deep bow.

GOOD NEWS

The story of the fight to protect the mustangs has a happy ending. It is now a federal offense to hunt wild horses on public lands or ranges from an airplane or a motor vehicle.

Much of the credit for bringing the mustangs' plight to Congressional attention belongs to Mrs. Velma B. Johnston of the Double Lazy Heart Ranch, Wadsworth, Nevada. Mrs. Johnston's struggle to get Congress to save the mustangs from extinction gained her the nickname of "Wild Horse Annie."